About the author

Tony was born and raised in Cambridgeshire. He studied History at Loughborough University as a mature student. After attending Exeter University he qualified as a teacher in 1989 and went on to be a successful history teacher in Somerset and Sussex until 2016. During his time in teaching he served as Head of History for 21 years. He was also a sixth form boarding housemaster for 13 years. He has now retired from the teaching profession to concentrate on his writing career. He now lives with his family in Chichester and Taunton. His interests include cricket and travel.

THE PUNKNOWLE PLOT

TONY PHILLIPS

THE PUNKNOWLE PLOT

Vanguard Press

VANGUARD PAPERBACK

© Copyright 2017
TONY PHILLIPS
Cover illustration by Zoe Landwehr

The right of Tony Phillips to be identified as author of this work has been asserted by him in accordance with the Copyright, Designs and Patents Act 1988.

All Rights Reserved

No reproduction, copy or transmission of this publication may be made without written permission.
No paragraph of this publication may be reproduced, copied or transmitted save with the written permission of the publisher, or in accordance with the provisions of the Copyright Act 1956 (as amended).

Any person who commits any unauthorised act in relation to this publication may be liable to criminal prosecution and civil claims for damages.

A CIP catalogue record for this title is available from the British Library.

ISBN 978 1 784652 47 0

Vanguard Press is an imprint of
Pegasus Elliot MacKenzie Publishers Ltd.
www.pegasuspublishers.com

First Published in 2017

Vanguard Press
Sheraton House Castle Park
Cambridge England

Printed & Bound in Great Britain

For my parents,
Elwyn and Irene Phillips,
To whom I owe everything.

1

I loathe train journeys especially in the winter months when the view from the dirty window is further obscured by the low glaring sun of early March. Commencing my trip at Taunton I was obliged to remove the remnants of a custard cream biscuit and a prawn cocktail crisp from the only available seat. An empty crisp packet on the floor had betrayed the identity of the offending item. Also there was a table in front of my seat upon which some individual, probably from the more exposed parts of rural Cornwall, had left a half-eaten chicken tikka sandwich. Sitting next to me was a large woman with a red nose who proceeded to sniff at regular intervals. The nose blowing was less regular but the pile of moistened tissues on the table would suggest a journey that had probably started at Penzance.

Opposite me sat a frumpy little chap aged around forty wearing a dark grey suit that had obviously spent many months stranded on a rail in a Marks and Spencer outlet store before being reduced for clearance. To his left sat a teenager with a threatening disposition. This youth was wearing the familiar livery of a football shirt and torn jeans. Wafting from his general direction was a heavy aroma of cheap scent. The tattoo on the inside of his left arm confirmed he was a Chelsea supporter. At thirty-five I was not exactly old myself but I detested young people, especially those who avoided wearing a collar and tie and a decent pair of brogues. I suppose it was this dislike of the youth of today that inspired me to become a teacher in the first place.

Of course this journey into the depths of East Anglia was forced upon me. I was going to attend an interview for the Head of History position at Lord Bilgebury College for Boys. I had to leave my last post at a prestigious private school, Picton College in Taunton, just after the start of the Spring Term. The Headmaster had taken exception to the fact that I had borrowed four hundred pounds from my boarding house funds. The money was required to purchase a new suit and he refused to believe it was my intention to return the amount borrowed in monthly instalments of ten pounds. The Picton Headmaster, however, had the nerve to call it theft and I was summarily dismissed for what was no more than a little creative accounting. Fortunately my Uncle Rex was Chairman of the governing board and therefore I was confident the episode would not be mentioned in any future references.

Having successfully protected myself from my neighbour's prolonged sneezing fit I proceeded to give some thought to the interview due to take place later that day at two o'clock. I have never liked interviews and certainly I have had some unfortunate experiences in the past few weeks. I attended one interview in the north of England and far too close to the proposed People's Republic of Scotland for my liking. There the Head had the nerve to ask me to leave simply because I made a trivial mistake with regard to my qualifications. On my curriculum vitae I suggested I had a PhD degree from Loughborough University. Upon investigation it seemed Loughborough had no record of the award. This may have been due to the fact that I had delayed the start of my research but it was my sincere intent to complete my PhD at some stage in the future. Therefore I was denied a job over a question of timing. Last week I went for an interview at a Catholic school in Bristol. The Head phoned me to say my application had been unsuccessful and that the priest observing my lower sixth lesson had been somewhat disturbed over my comment that Henry VIII should have closed down more monasteries. Only two days ago I was turned down for a job in Dorchester. Some old bore on the interview panel wanted to know if I'd read the latest biography on Herbert Hoover. I explained that I was a historian and manuals on domestic cleaning appliances didn't really interest me. Obviously my interviewer had a sense of humour failure.

The fellow opposite was obviously uneasy about the youth sitting next to him. Leaning to his left he was attempting to ensure there was no physical contact so as not to provoke a verbal or even violent response. Certainly the long haired individual appeared capable of train rage. The more respectable gentleman then proceeded to take some papers out of his black leather executive briefcase. While reading one sheet of paper he laid the rest in a neat pile upon the table. I couldn't believe my eyes.

The train pulled into Reading Station and fortunately it was time for the football hooligan to alight. The Marks and Spencer attired gent nervously made way for the Chelsea supporter and as the vicious looking lout left he reached up for his Oxford University sweat shirt and a book on applied mathematics. The woman beside me remained in her seat and continued to sniff and add to the ever growing papier-mache mountain.

On leaving Reading I decided to make the first move. The man opposite had in his possession the same glossy material Lord Bilgebury College had sent me the week previously. Without doubt he was another candidate for the History post.

'Excuse me but do you happen to know what time we get into Paddington?' The red nosed lady turned toward me but fortunately my fellow interviewee was the first to respond. 'I believe we're due in at nine thirty five, or at least that's what the timetable says.'

'That will be around ten then?'

Consulting his watch he assured me we would be just about on time. He then continued to peruse the glossy pages of his Lord Bilgebury pile. I had been particularly amused when I looked through the school brochure before throwing it into the waste paper bin. There had been numerous pictures of pupils being taught by a teacher in a classroom; perhaps not very original. Public examination results did not appear in the publication, which rather suggested the College had something to hide with regard to its record on academic attainment.

'Well I hope it's on time as I've got to get across London for a connection.' Although he gave me a reassuring smile, I sensed a degree of irritation on his part. He was obviously eager to continue with his preparation for the interview. However, I persisted.

'Yes, I need to be in Cambridge by two o'clock.' At last I detected some interest in his eyes.

'Oh really,' he said, placing all of his papers on the table, 'I'm actually going to Cambridge myself. There's a train from

Liverpool Street at eleven so you should be ok. It only takes just over an hour to get from there to Cambridge.'

'I have some business there', I said keeping my real intentions to close to my chest, 'And yourself?'

With a little hesitation he confirmed what I already knew, 'I've got an interview for a position at a school in Cambridge, as Head of the History Department.'

'Really? How interesting', I replied keeping my cover intact, 'the name's Plantagenet by the way, Richard Plantagenet.' This was an alias as I wanted to hide my true identity; my real name was Sebastian Punknowle. Also, a more regal name had always held some appeal.

Waiting for our fellow traveller to complete yet another nasal blow out and thus add to the mountain range amassing before us, he introduced himself as 'Brian Fagg.'

'So what time is your interview?'

'The process starts at three o'clock; I'm meeting with the Head and a few other senior members of staff.'

'And the school in question?'

'It's Lord Bilgebury College, a small independent school not too far from the station thankfully. And what line of business are you in Mr Plantagenet?'

His query caught me a little off guard as I was contemplating my next probing question. 'I work for the Royal Bank of Scotland in the credit card section.' I had received a nasty letter this morning from the bank threatening to take me to court for not sending the monthly minimum repayment on my credit card. I was currently in debt to the tune of around eight thousand pounds. In fact I had debts all over the place and since losing my job at Picton College I have had to restrict myself to one bottle of the less expensive brands of champagne every evening.

My broad pin-striped navy suit seemed to confirm my line of work. Becoming more familiar Fagg made reference to the student who had departed the train at Reading. 'Obviously standards have dropped at Oxford. He's probably at Wadham', he pronounced knowingly with a wry grin.

'A village near Oxford?'

'No, no, no', he replied with a slight chuckle, 'it's where the less bright sparks tend to go. It's also one of the more financially endowed colleges if you understand my meaning', he exclaimed with another grin. 'I was up at Exeter myself.'

'Oh I know Exeter very well indeed. A friend of mine went there to study Engineering. Yes, he failed to make it to his second year; too much time spent on the beach at Exmouth in the summer term me thinks.' This geographical reference to the county of Devon caused Fagg to stop smiling and looked at me with a degree of contempt.

Rather pompously Fagg informed me that he was referring to Exeter College, Oxford. Fagg was obviously going to pose a threat to me getting the job at Bilgebury, especially as he also casually informed me that he wrote articles for *History Review,* a prestigious magazine for A level students. The rather ordinary, if somewhat fictional, features of my own curriculum vitae began to occupy my mind as we approached Paddington Station. Fagg collected together his Lord Bilgebury papers and returned them to his case while the woman next to me un-wrapped her sixth lozenge in as many minutes.

Fagg and I agreed to journey to Cambridge together and when we arrived at Paddington at ten forty we made our way straight to the Underground. While we were still on the main platform making for the exit I couldn't help but notice that about ten yards in front of us was the large lady with the red nose. Still engaged in her prolonged fit of sneezing she caught the attention of other travellers who were making their way to other parts of the realm.

I assumed the Circle Line serving Paddington was always busy, but it was very busy for the time of the morning. Obviously those idle bank workers didn't get into their offices until nearly lunch time. Was it any wonder the country was in the mess it's in? However, the bustle and the heaving crowd of commuters suited my purpose perfectly.

I deliberately left it to Fagg to direct us to the right platform; I was quite content to remain just behind him. The Circle Line went directly to Liverpool Street and therefore there was no need to change lines. The overhead electronic information system informed us the next train was due in two minutes. People continued to pile on to an already crowded platform. As the train approached, Fagg was by the edge of the platform. I was just behind him.

2

The taxi from Paddington to Liverpool Street had delayed my journey; the array of emergency services vehicles converging on Paddington didn't exactly help but I still managed to arrive in Cambridge in good time.

I thought there was no need to arrive at Lord Bilgebury too early so I walked the short distance to the city centre. Cambridge seemed an odd place at first sight. Shops, restaurants and building societies mingled with famous old University colleges. Also, there were blasted bikes everywhere. Astride these velocipedes were students with a certain air of superiority and wearing university scarves as if to prove they were not ordinary mortals.

From the market I crossed the street to King's College with its world famous chapel. A miserable chap in a dark suit and bowler hat looking like an undertaker tried to relieve me of four pounds when I tried to enter the College grounds. I didn't remember having to pay such a sum to go through the main gate at Luton Poly so I made a sneering retreat. Crossing the street once more proved to be a hazardous affair. It was those damn bikes again. This time there was a whole load of them. It was like the Japanese army advancing with haste through Malaya. Running across the road I had to endure the humiliation of having several bicycle bells rung at me. A horn was also blasted by an undergraduate in a light blue scarf. On a market stall I found exactly what I was looking for. Returning to the site, which had only a few moments ago represented a frantic scene in the Tour de Yorkshire, I sprinkled a box of drawing pins all over the road. Revenge was sweet!

Having successfully hailed a taxi on King's Parade I soon found myself at the main entrance of Lord Bilgebury College. The main doors were at the bottom of a square central stone tower with a flag pole on top. Either side of the tower were connecting wings with large windows surrounded by ivy. It was difficult to put a date on the construction of the building as it was part mock Elizabethan manor, part castle and part church. I therefore deduced it was built at some stage during the reign of Queen Victoria. Half way up the tower was a round blue clock with gold dials which displayed the correct time of two forty-five.

Just inside the entrance was a sign giving directions to Reception where I was to report upon arrival. I rang a bell by the side of a half open stable door and within seconds a rather attractive young woman appeared. I would have put her in her late twenties. A red dress showed off her trim figure and the colour of her frock complimented her free flowing blonde hair. She was entirely aware she was being stared at. 'Can I help you', she asked with a smile.

'Yes I hope so. I'm Sebastian Punknowle. I'm here for the Head of History position.'

'Ah yes Mr Punknowle, I'm Lucy Dockett, the Head's Personal Assistant. You're due to see Walter, I mean the Headmaster, at three forty five. You'll be meeting the Chaplain first at around three fifteen. I'll take you to where the other candidates are waiting.' The informal reference to the Headmaster was not lost on me.

'Ok, thanks very much.' I then followed her down the corridor where the smell of wood polish was strong. Certainly, the parquet flooring appeared to be immaculate. As we progressed she continued with the small talk.

'I understand you've come all the way from Taunton', she asked with apparent interest.

'Yes, that's right.'

'We were expecting another candidate from Plymouth, but he has yet to arrive.'

There was no need to respond as I was shown into a room where two men and a woman were talking. Here was the opposition. These people stood between me and getting the job I so desperately needed.

I was parched and feeling a little hungry and therefore before making their acquaintance I piled into the posh continental biscuits and poured myself a cup of coffee. Four lumps of sugar were added to give me strength for the impending experience. As I walked over to the other candidates, one of the chaps detached himself from the group to present his credentials.

'Hello my name is Tom Wisbeach. Have you come far?'

'Taunton, so quite a way. Sebastian Punknowle. Nice to meet you.' I offered my hand, which he accepted with a firm grasp. For me he was the enemy and not unlike Napoleon Bonaparte I immediately set out to discover any weaknesses. 'So where do you teach at the moment?' I was hoping he was going to come up with some third rate educational establishment.

'I'm the second in department at Marlborough College, and you?'

My heart sank, but almost at once I replied that I was between jobs. He looked at me as if he knew; I was there because I needed a job and that he was there as a matter of destiny. He was good looking, well dressed and at least eight inches taller than me. An inferiority complex was starting to weaken my resolve, but the nerd-like creature across the room gave me cause for hope. Keeping my eyes on the Marlborough foe I walked towards the other candidates. Marlborough followed.

'Hello, Sebastian. Nice to meet you.' The nerd was in his late twenties and wearing a green corduroy suit, check shirt and plain dark brown tie. The knot of the tie was attempting, unsuccessfully, to hide the lack of a top button on his shirt. His greasy dark brown hair was parted on the left and only a double crown loosened the controlling effect of the limp unwashed hair. A cheap pair of brown rimmed glasses hung precariously from his ears and the end of his nose. The woman looked as if she was the youngest person ever to be appointed as a Justice of the Peace. No older than about thirty she dressed liked someone nearing retirement. She wore her hair in a way that Maria would have been proud of before becoming Frau von Trapp. Certainly, the low heeled shoes would have completed the alpine trek from Austria to Switzerland with rubber to spare.

The nerd acknowledged me first. The magistrate looked at me as if she had just sent me down for six months for indecent exposure and then started to strike up a conversation with Marlborough.

'Boyle, Edward Boyle.' As we were shaking hands I could not help but notice the large red spot on his neck.

'How appropriate', I said still staring at the red bulge that so desperately wanted to erupt.

'What is?'

'Oh no matter.' It transpired that the nerd had been teaching in some awful comprehensive in Leeds. This was hardly the right sort of preparation for a post at Lord Bilgebury College. Also, he didn't offer rugger or cricket. Not even badminton appeared on his curriculum vitae. However, I could leave nothing to chance. 'Coffee Edward?' The nerd accepted my offer and so I went over to the corner of the room to pour him a cup from the cafetiere.

The nerd drank his coffee but appeared to wince after the first gulp. Miss Dockett re-entered the room, smiled and proceeded to give us our individual itineraries. Marlborough was going on a tour of the College, the nerd was off to see the Head of History, the magistrate was starting with the Head, and I was to be received as expected by the College Chaplain. As we left base camp I had a discreet word with Marlborough. 'Well, you can see she fancies you.'

'Who?'

'Our Miss Dockett of course. Surely you could see the way she was looking at you?' He hadn't and neither had I come to that. It was, however, the start of the ploy to rid the field of the most serious threat. Certainly, Marlborough lost no time in making eyes at the personal assistant who was obviously deserving of his amorous attentions. There had been no time to assess the magistrate but if my instincts were correct she would not pose a problem.

I was assigned a sixth form pupil and he led me through a series of corridors along yet more highly polished wooden floors. One had to be careful when turning a corner in order to avoid the same fate as an Olympic ice skater who did not win a medal. We stopped in front of a door which had 'RE 2' above it. The pupil produced a limp knock. He did not wait for a response and opened the door to reveal a clergyman sitting in an armchair by a dormant fireplace.

'Hello', he said with some enthusiasm, 'Do come in Mr...er...', he reached for his paperwork on a coffee table, '...Mr Punknowle.' He offered me the only other armchair in the room. Although he didn't introduce himself I knew from the College literature that his name was Augustine Slabb. In order to break the ice I remarked that his room didn't look like a traditional classroom.

'My dear boy, I don't teach the little ones. No, I leave that to Miss Friggis. I tend only to give guidance to the A-level RE students. Yes, they come here for little chats about the great philosophical issues and other such matters related to their studies.' He rambled on and I realized that the Chaplain, at least for the time being, was content to talk about himself. Slabb told me that he had been at the College for fifteen years and before that he had been engaged in missionary work in South America. He was a portly chap with a round face topped by silver hair. Although it was not warm in his room he was constantly mopping sweat from his brow. Aged about sixty, or at least approaching it, he wore an off-white dog collar and judging by the remnants on his shirt he had enjoyed spaghetti bolognaise for lunch. His grey herringbone jacket had obviously seen better times with the lapels seeming to have a mind of their own and a tendency to curl inwards. Even when pausing during his monologue his mouth appeared to be permanently open thus revealing teeth that had not been prodded with dental instruments for a considerable time.

'Would you be prepared to give the odd sermon in Chapel? Most of our masters are happy to do at least one a year.' The interview had officially begun. I responded in the affirmative with a mental image of myself acting the part of a very convincing Ian Paisley in the pulpit. He asked his next question with some passion as if the future of the world depended on it. 'Do you play cricket Mr…er…?' This time he didn't reach for his information sheet and instead appeared to grip his knee caps tightly. He revealed a broad smile when once again I produced a positive answer. The rest of the interview was taken up by the future of test cricket and the drawbacks of the twenty-twenty format. When Miss Dockett came to collect me for my session with the Headmaster I had every reason to feel satisfied with stage one.

'We'll go through the motions Tim, but she's not for us.' I wasn't supposed to hear this but the door to the Headmaster's study was slightly ajar when I was waiting just outside. I assumed the Headmaster was talking about the magistrate. I thought very probably that physically she didn't quite fit the bill. This was encouraging because the next stage of my master plan depended on my belief that the Headmaster of Lord Bilgebury College was someone who appreciated pretty young ladies. Obviously the magistrate had not sent a photograph with her application.

I was shown in to the Headmaster's study by Miss Dockett. After announcing me she went through to an anteroom, which served as her office. The Headmaster never took his eyes off her until she was out of sight. His eyes were fixed particularly on her shapely bottom and legs. 'Thank you Lucy.'

She turned and smiled, 'My pleasure Headmaster.' He too smiled and I knew then I was right.

Walter Grover-Smythe, Headmaster of Lord Bilgebury College since 1998, was your typical independent school head. His MSc in Business Management would suggest that he had attempted to make up for a mediocre degree from a mediocre university. Very probably he had been an average teacher of Geography who, after three or four years, had been appointed as a boarding housemaster. With an absence of scandal he would have successfully applied for a deputy headship. After four or five years of drawing up lists, organizing detentions and faithfully supporting his leader he was at last able to assume command in his own right. This was not guess work; Uncle Rex had obtained for me from a few chums all the information deemed necessary for a successful outcome to the interview process at Lord Bilgebury College.

At over six feet and in his mid fifties he was as bald as a billiard ball and there was an air of pomposity, another characteristic associated with headship. Indeed his entire bearing reminded one of Benito Mussolini in his prime. He wore a black pin-stripe suit with a waistcoat; this was a deliberate ploy to indicate that he had left teaching and was now engaged in the world of high finance and business.

The Headmaster's study was wood panelled, broken only by a mock Tudor fireplace above which hung a picture of the College as it looked in 1925 when it celebrated its centenary year. In addition to four leather armchairs there were two Chesterfield sofas either side of the fireplace. Other items of furniture included a desk, a large bookshelf containing a number of texts from the Bournemouth Business School, a filing cabinet and a drinks cabinet – all mahogany.

'Good afternoon Mr Punknowle', and pointing to the man, with rodent-like features, sitting to the left of his partner's desk, 'This is Tim Ferris, our Director of Studies. He'll be sitting in on the interview.' I nodded my acceptance of the situation.

'I understand you're on a sabbatical at the moment?' Obviously Uncle Rex had done his stuff and now I simply had to think on my feet. 'So tell us what you've been doing with yourself.'

'I've actually been writing a historical novel set during the English Civil War.' The blank expressions from both interviewers suggested I was on safe ground.

'How very interesting.' He ventured no further with my project. He did, however, proceed to ask all the usual tedious and predictable questions. My responses were I felt adequate, but I wasn't quite sure what the rodent was scribbling on his yellow legal pad. It occurred to me that he was recording my every word and that during the evening he would use my responses as evidence against me. This was part paranoia but also the fear that Marlborough would put on a sparkling performance whilst sitting in this very chair. I was saved by the reappearance of Miss Dockett who had returned to remind the Headmaster that his next interview was scheduled to begin in five minutes. She retreated to her office once more. 'I have to say Headmaster that Miss Dockett seems to be a very charming lady.'

'Yes she is and very efficient with it.'

'And seems to make friends and admirers very quickly.'

'Admirers, what do you mean Mr Punknowle?'

'Well I'm sure if Mr Wisbeach secured the position it wouldn't be long before he and Miss Dockett were an item.'

'An item?' The Headmaster was becoming agitated.

'It's just that I know Mr Wisbeach finds her very attractive and I did see them chatting and joking together. Love at first sight and that sort of thing.'

The Headmaster looked pale, the rodent beside him simply looked confused.

A College Prefect collected me from the Headmaster's study and was directed by the rodent to take me to see the incumbent Head of History. The blazer of the Prefect was obviously a symbol of rank – dark green with gold braid following the edges of the lapels. On the breast pocket there was an elaborate College emblem. He looked like an Australian test cricketer in official tour garb. I think he believed himself to be superior, looking at other pupils as if they were mere England cricketers who had just been subjected to yet another mauling at the hands of the old enemy from down under.

The Head of History, Peter Nesbitt, was moving on to become the Head of Sixth Form in a school in North Wales. I wondered what possible misdemeanor he could have committed to be sent to such a bleak outpost of the realm. Surely nobody, certainly not an Englishman, would actually choose to go to Wales. Perhaps male voice choirs and rain represented some form of morbid attraction. He informed me the department had achieved success in terms of exam results but recently there had been disappointment over GCSE and A level recruitment numbers. Detailing the chosen syllabus content it was obvious, at least to me, why History was not a popular option. In my experience pupils enjoyed learning about kings and queens and wars. Personally I was a great admirer of Napoleon Bonaparte. Nesbitt had made them study social history and delved into topics such as prostitution in nineteenth century India. I felt somehow that GCSE candidates would not be turned on by issues like poverty in Peterborough during the 1780s lettuce famine.

Nesbitt's description of the other members of the History Department was also revealing. 'There are two other members of the department. Arnold Pryke is our medieval specialist but unfortunately has a problem with classroom discipline', No surprise there I thought, 'You should know that Arnold is in his fifties and is looking for early retirement. He's finding it too much of a strain. He missed lunch last week because his Year 9 group tied his ankles to his desk; it was the final straw, especially as his Year 6 class after lunch refused to release him from his bondage.' What do you expect when eleven year olds are subjected to life in a medieval monastery? 'Guy Straker on the other hand is a popular young teacher. The kids love him, an excellent rapport with the sixth form and a real asset to the department. We're lucky to have him.' If I was appointed he'd have to go.

On my way back to the candidate assembly point I saw Marlborough emerge from the Headmaster's study. He was visibly shaken. 'Everything alright old boy?' I asked with total insincerity.

'No, not really.' He was trembling and looked as if his entire world had fallen apart.

'Why, what's happened?' I tried to appear sympathetic.

'Well I've just been given a really rough time by Grover-Smythe. He practically accused me of harassing that secretary of his. I had only asked her about arranging a taxi to the station, but he refused to believe me. I couldn't work here; he's bonkers, completely off his trolley.'

He was due to see the Chaplain at that point, but instead he made for the front door.

In the meantime the interview merry-go-round had broken down because the nerd had gone missing. However, he had recently been located by the Head of Science asleep in the male staff lavatory. The Headmaster had assumed the nerd was suffering from some form of soporific condition and sent his loyal rodent, the Ferret, to ask him to leave. The drug in the coffee had achieved its objective.

The process was over by four thirty. The tour of the College had been most encouraging. I was relieved to discover that the College had pupils, classrooms and teachers. The Headmaster had no cause to consider further his decision. I was offered the post of Head of History at Lord Bilgebury College for Boys. I duly accepted.

While waiting for my train at Cambridge station I picked up the local rag, *The Cambridge Evening News.* The headlines came as no real surprise: 'PADDINGTON UNDERGROUND ACCIDENT.'

3

It was the first Sunday of September and the boarders were due to arrive in the afternoon at various times after three o'clock. I arrived at Lord Bilgebury the previous Tuesday to prepare for the new job. In addition to the Head of History position I agreed to take on the role of resident assistant in a boarding house. During the 1930s the great-grandson of Lord Bilgebury, the Right Honourable Sir Willoughby Bilgebury, had served in the Stanley Baldwin government. Later in 1938, as Chairman of the Board of Governors, he decreed that each boarding house should be named after some of his fellow cabinet members. Hence today there is a Baldwin House, Chamberlain House, Halifax House, Swinton House and Eden House. It was my misfortune to have been attached to the boarding house named after Sir Samuel Hoare.

My accommodation was of modest size. I got up from the two-seater sofa last night and very nearly put my right knee through my new plasma TV screen. My portrait of Margaret Thatcher just about took up one wall and on the book shelf there was only enough space for my original edition of Mein Kampf and the biographies on Hitler, Napoleon Bonaparte and Bismarck. The kitchen only had space for a sink, small fridge and one of those Belling miniature cookers. There will be no opportunity to sip a glass of Bollinger in the bath due to the fact there wasn't one. I had a temperamental shower that was either too hot or too cold. The bedroom was also tiny with a window that looked directly across to the Maths Department.

In the mornings I usually had to make a hasty retreat from the shower as the water was just about at boiling point as was my temper with the plumbing arrangements. One morning just prior to the start of term, while having my shave in my domestic steam room, I gave some consideration to my long term career objectives. By the time I had finished shaving the left side of my face I had decided upon a plan of action. It was my intention to become Headmaster of Lord Bilgebury College. To achieve my objective would take careful planning and cunning but I was sure I was up to the task. Over the next year or so I would have to rid the College of any likely contenders and make myself indispensable as far as the governing board was concerned.

I had met some of the contenders the previous Friday in the staff inset. The rodent-like Director of Studies, Tim Ferris, and who I had dubbed the 'Ferret' during the interview gave us an uninspiring talk on pupil tracking. He was rambling on about strategies to be adopted for children who were failing. My philosophy on the matter was always to let the malignant youths fail. However, as I listened to him droning on I realized that exam success had to be part of my strategy. The Ferret had been at the College for ten years and was highly regarded so he would have to be dispatched without delay. Obviously the main target for disposal was the Deputy Head, David Fotheringay. Aged thirty-four he was a high-flier and destined for great things such as a headship in one of England's premier independent schools. However, I didn't want him getting any leadership experience at Lord Bilgebury College. He had graduated from Oxford with first-class honours in English Literature, was suave in his appearance and obviously had the respect of the Senior Common Room. It was enough to make you want to vomit.

Another threat to my plans was the Housemaster of Hoare House, Dr Donald Read. For reasons that were beyond me I was the first of his colleagues ever to refer to him as 'Doctor Dread.' He was also the Economics master, which rather suited his somewhat dreary character. However, I considered him a possible problem because by all accounts he represented a safe pair of hands. He was also a Methodist and as Lord Bilgebury College was a Methodist school he would certainly appeal to the traditionalists on the governing board should the headship become vacant. Furthermore, his wife's brother was one of those traditionalists on the board of governors. In the meantime should he depart, as his assistant in Hoare House, I would be well placed to take on the job as housemaster, a recognized stepping stone to headship.

The rest of the inset was made up of a first aid course and fire extinguisher training. I took no particular interest in either. In my experience it was better to let someone expire rather than give first aid. Firstly, there was the real risk of catching something unpleasant whilst administering the kiss of life. Secondly, if first aid was given and something went wrong there was always the lawyer in the deceased person's family who wanted to take you to the cleaners in the county court. It simply made more sense to ignore the groaning and cries for help and walk straight past. With regard to a fire I was not going to be the mug left behind fighting a blaze when everyone else was making for the fire exits. If I'd wanted a career as a fireman I would have joined the Fire Brigade. However, I did have tremendous fun when I accidently drenched the Head of English with carbon dioxide foam and proceeded to drop the empty extinguisher on his foot. Fortunately there were plenty of newly trained first aiders on hand.

At the end of the inset day the Headmaster addressed the staff in the rather modest Assembly Hall, comparing unfavourably with the grandeur of Picton College's Great Hall. Not unlike Mussolini in a suit, he attempted to impress us with his business acumen. He took us through a power point presentation which detailed financial forecasts and ambitious building projects. By the time we got to the building issues the Chaplain had dozed off although Dr Dread was taking detailed notes for the benefit of his wife. The plans included a new assembly hall that would double as a performing arts centre. However, plans for a new cricket pavilion were dropped. The Chaplain awoke from his slumber with a loud snort; the word 'cricket' normally breathed new life into Augustine Slabb. The Headmaster also mentioned public examination results and it was clear he wanted to see an improvement in this area. He cited the boy who walked out of a Physics exam last summer because he claimed to be an orange. As oranges didn't take exams he saw no point in staying in the exam hall. The History results were poor; prostitution in nineteenth century India did not feature in the exam paper and as predicted nobody was particularly inspired by poverty in Peterborough. I was determined to make sure all History candidates passed their exams next year.

At the end of his address the Headmaster introduced the new Domestic Bursar, the woman to be in charge of cooking, cleaning and other menial tasks. Angelica Smite

was of stern appearance and looked as if she had been acquitted, just, by the Nuremburg War Trials Commission in 1946. Certainly, she looked a formidable female and one you didn't cross if you wanted to avoid being bludgeoned by a rolling pin. I was the only other new arrival on the staff although the Head didn't seem to think I was significant enough to warrant a mention.

On Sunday afternoon Dr Dread and I were in the Hoare House Common Room waiting for the new Year 9 arrivals and those boarders who were returning from last year. Dread's wife, Gloria, was in her own kitchen preparing an array of nibbles and savouries for the parents who were dropping off their offspring. Gloria Read was obviously an ambitious woman who was constantly cajoling and bullying her husband. When I met her for the first time the previous week, she made it perfectly clear that her husband was destined for high office. From what I had seen she chose her friends with great care. If they couldn't be used to help propel her husband to greatness they were surplus to requirements. Mrs Grover-Smythe was thought to be her best friend; I had been made to feel like the last entry in the surplus column.

The first person to arrive was the Head of House, Wayne Flack. He wasn't wearing a prefect's blazer nor even a suit or jacket. Instead he was decked out in a leather motorbike jacket, a torn black t-shirt with some offensive wording, camouflaged combat trousers with the 'waist' starting half way down his backside above which you could see the waist band of his

Calvin Klein briefs. I was also a little surprised that a pupil was permitted to have a shaved head and an ear stud. While he was getting changed into something more respectable Dr Dread explained Flack's background, 'He's a bit of a rebel really, and I see him very much as my mission this year. His father ran off when he was very young leaving the mother to bring him up. I'm afraid she's an alcoholic and can't really cope with Wayne. The grandparents seem to have him most times during the holidays. I think the whole family is a bit rough actually; I believe his grandfather ran a market stall in the east end of London. I think he was quite successful; it's the grandfather who pays the fees. According to the Bursar the fees are always paid promptly and in cash. There was never any chance the Headmaster was going to make him a prefect - caught smoking too many times for that. And of course he's been a bit of a bully in his time. Yes, I remember the occasion he put a dead rat behind a boy's radiator. The wretched thing wasn't discovered for weeks and before we were aware of the origin of the odour we had sent the poor lad for tests at Addenbrooke's Hospital. We only discovered it was Flack who planted the rat when he was overheard boasting about it.' I had assumed correctly that the Director of Studies had not been the one stuffed behind the radiator.

'So why did you make him the Head of Hoare', I asked sensing a certain empathy with my own experiences as a child at school.

'Well I suppose I wanted to give him a chance, to see if a bit of responsibility would mend his ways. I know it's a big gamble, and the Head has warned me that any more trouble and he'll be expelled. Gloria is far from happy with the appointment. But the lad has given me his word.' The experience of Neville Chamberlain dealing with Hitler at Munich sprang to mind. However, if Dr Dread were to be successful in his endeavour to turn Flack around then that would represent another feather in the good Doctor's cap.

Trying to discover another logical explanation as to why this thug had been raised up I asked if he had a sporting talent.

'Oh no, he doesn't play any sport. He was a good bowler but he rather blotted his copy book last year in an effort to get a match cancelled so he could attend a rock concert at the Corn Exchange. He hasn't played for the College since. The cricketers, and even the Chaplain, have never forgiven him for digging up the First XI pitch the night before the match against Saffron Walden College; a very important date on the fixture list – bit of a grudge match.'

'In the CCF then?'

'Well he was, at least until the unfortunate abseiling incident.'

'Abseiling incident?'

'Yes, Wayne was on top of the CCF abseiling frame at a summer camp a couple of years ago. His job was to attach the rope to the cadet's belts before sending them over the edge. Well he dropped one boy from the top of the frame.'

'So what was wrong with that?'

'No rope!'

Dr Dread did not notice my slight grin. I liked the sound of this lad Flack. I thought I might have a use for him. There was still no sign of any more arrivals so I decided to go back to my flat to collect a pen I had left behind. As I was coming out of the Common Room I saw Flack in the corridor going through the contents of a black handbag. I assumed it belonged to Gloria Read as it was on a table just outside the housemaster's office. Instead of stopping him in his tracks I allowed Flack to continue. He was unaware of two things. First I was observing him from just behind the door frame, and secondly he was being recorded on the recently installed CCTV. He proceeded to lift a twenty pound note from the bag. This criminal activity on the part of Flack encouraged me greatly. I had no intention of interrupting his activities but the matter would be addressed a little later.

The first new boy to arrive was Albert Noggins and unlike Flack he was attired in his new uniform of navy blazer and charcoal trousers. His shirt collar was too big for him and it was obvious that the Windsor knot in his red and white striped tie had been crafted by his father. For a thirteen-year-old he was somewhat physically undeveloped; in a word he looked like a wimp and a likely candidate to be Flack's first victim. I had to pretend that I cared about the little worm and assured him that all would be well. I also had to endure the usual small talk with his parents, as I did with the other parents who arrived that afternoon. One always had the impression they felt they paid your salary and for this generous act of philanthropy they expected you to put up with tiresome summer holiday stories. There was always the usual 'we must have you over for dinner' invitation, which roughly translated into please look after their son; you might at some stage get an invite but don't hold your breath. Worse of all was the father who thought he was a born again historian because he's managed to read two chapters of the latest Simon Schama book. I particularly dreaded the parent who claimed an interest in the

Second World War. This usually meant they had started to collect magazines on weekly basis, and the plastic model of a *Spitfire* that accompanied it. Some had perhaps even joined a military history book club. The books had normally been selected not because of the quality of the content but by the attractiveness of the cover. As a History teacher I tended to read a wide range of history books on various topics. I have a particular passion for nineteenth century European history, especially the history of France, Germany and Italy. I tended to teach Italian unification during January and February on the basis it cheered me up during these dreary and lifeless months. However, Hollywood and Pinewood Studios also provided much of the information my pupils needed. *'The Hamilton Woman'* and *'Waterloo'* are particular favourites. As long as they left school knowing that the British always beat the French and the Germans that would suffice.

Most of the boarders had returned by six o'clock. As they made their way to the tender care of Miss Smite in the dining hall I kept Flack behind. 'I won't keep you long Flack, just wanted to have a little chat.' He was no longer in his thug gear. He was now in a black suit wearing a black shirt and white tie; he looked like a member of the mob. He was eager to have his supper.

'Can it wait sir? I could do with some grub.'

'Not really Flack. Not if you want to remain at this School.'

'What d'you mean?'

'Well Flack, it's about the twenty pounds you took from Mrs Read's handbag.'

'I didn't nick nothin'.' I excused the double negative.

'Ah but I saw you Flack, as did the CCTV.' He looked at the wall and saw a camera.

'I'll put it back sir, promise I will.'

'If I tell the Head about this, you'll be expelled will you not?'

'Suppose so.'

'Tell you what Flack, you keep the money.'

'You what?'

'Exactly what I said, keep the twenty pounds'

'I don't get it; you mean you're not goin' to dob me in?' He couldn't believe his luck.

'That's right Flack.'

'Cheers sir, but I don't get it.'

'Well Flack let's put it this way. You now work for me and from this point on you do exactly as I say. You put a foot wrong and I'll take this matter to the Headmaster. Understand?'

'You're not queer or anythin' are ya?'

'No Flack', I replied a little irritated by his line of questioning.

'Well what sort of things do ya want me to do then?'

'We can discuss the details later. Do we have a deal or not?'

'Yeh why not; it's a deal.'

'Good. Now off you go for your supper and remember Flack, not a word to anyone about this. Understood?'

'Understood.'

I was gracious enough to erase the theft scene from the camera file on the computer so that Dr Dread was unaware of the misdemeanor. There was another reason why Flack could have been made up to Head of House. None of the other members of the upper sixth showed any leadership potential. Some were destined for some decent red bricks and no doubt some could put up a bit of a fight when it came to chess, but I detected for the most part Hoare House was devoid of fellows with any capacity for life in the fast lane. Not one of them played cricket, a serious omission in a child's development. But Flack was different and it was touching to see him talking to young Noggins who was having trouble settling in.

'What's wrong with you No Mates?'

'I want to go home.'

'You'll go to hell with a kick in the teeth if you don't shut up.'

Yes, Flack was the right choice after all.

4

My first few weeks in the classroom passed without much incident. The National Curriculum was ignored and the scheme of study followed by the whole department reflected my own interests. There was no room for social and economic history. Books on local Cambridgeshire history were burned; I simply wasn't interested in teaching topics such as witchcraft in Whittlesford in the Middle Ages. Instead the department was instructed to study the great men of history – Napoleon Bonaparte, Bismarck and Churchill. If the teachers wanted to delve into a bit of modern history they were permitted to teach the life and times of Margaret Thatcher, the regime of Saddam Hussain and the presidency of George W. Bush.

Arnold Pryke, the old timer in the department seeking early retirement, was not at ease with my regime. It had come to my attention that he had sought advice on his pension settlement and applied for a job as a shelf filler at the local Tesco. It suited my objectives to have Pryke stay on; beside the old idiot I looked quite competent. Without naming myself I phoned the personnel department at Tesco to suggest that Pryke had a record of petty theft and therefore represented a risk to the company's profits. He wasn't invited for interview. Also, as the pension settlement fell short of what he wanted he decided to stay on at the College.

Guy Straker was a completely different kettle of fish. He was one of those types who genuinely believed teaching was his vocation. Everybody adored him – the pupils, his colleagues, the Head and even Angelica Smite had taken a shine to 'boy wonder.' He objected to my scheme of study preferring instead the politically biased National Curriculum. The pompous little creep also had the nerve to complain to the Deputy Head and the Ferret. I had the distinct impression that they were sympathetic to his view point. He was dangerous and his very presence in the College undermined my authority.

However, by half term he had been suspended pending an inquiry. It turned out he was a member of a far right political organization and this link was rightly unacceptable to the College. The Headmaster had no idea however that I was behind his membership. It was I who joined the organization using his name. As he lived at the College all his mail was delivered to his pigeon hole in the Senior Common Room. Early each morning for a week I went to check the content of Straker's pigeon hole. One envelope I opened contained the *History Monthly* magazine; it was dispatched to the recycling bin. As expected a plain brown envelope eventually appeared in his post. His name and address had obviously been written by a simpleton; it looked as if someone who was right-handed had used their left hand. The pack had arrived and attached to the information sheet was a covering letter welcoming Straker to the 'People's National Party of Britain'. All I had to do then was to leave the letter and other sheets in the Senior Common Room photocopier. The material was discovered by Daisy Dingle of the Maths Department. A sense of professionalism obliged her to take it to a very disappointed Deputy Head. Of course Straker denied any involvement in the PNPB but as I explained to the Headmaster that was to be expected. He would hardly admit to being a member of a racist organisation. The PNPB could not deny that Straker was a member, even if they wanted to. They had received a letter from Straker and they had simply responded by sending him an information pack. Also, there was a danger that the press would get hold of it. I asked the Headmaster to imagine what the *Daily Reflector* would have done with the story. I managed to persuade the College management that it was in the best interest of the College that Straker should at least be suspended from his duties. There was also the matter of no smoke without fire and that it would be better for Straker to go quietly and thus give himself the opportunity of finding alternative employment in a remote corner of the realm where the PNPB doesn't operate. I noticed in the most recent edition of the *Times Educational Supplement* that Inverness High School was looking for a humanities teacher.

Away from the political activities of my former colleague Uncle Rex did his best to help me out in my new position. I invited him across to address my lower sixth about his wartime experiences. Entitled *Rex Punknowle: My part in the overthrow of the Third Reich,* my uncle's lecture managed to slightly exaggerate his involvement in the Second World War. He made it seem as if he had single-handedly bombed Germany into submission. I calculated that he must have been aged seven when he took part in the Dam Busters raid. More than one eyebrow was raised when he claimed to have completed a victory roll over Buckingham Palace in his

Lancaster bomber on VE Day. Good old Uncle Rex; he could always be relied upon.

My most pressing task for the term was to rid Hoare House of its housemaster and to be appointed in his place. It would have been too risky to employ the same technique that had accounted for the demise of Straker. Read's reputation was beyond reproach and he had powerful supporters on the Board of Governors. Gloria Read had made sure of that. The Headmaster rated him very highly and regarded Read as a faithful confidant. I decided an accident would be necessary.

Since we came to an understanding Wayne Flack and I had forged a good relationship. I introduced him to the delights of whisky although I kept the malts to myself. Nor was he permitted to sample my inexpensive champagne or *Petit Chablis* and he had to make do with some cheap Italian sparkling wine. We enjoyed some good evenings whereby he described in detail how he tormented and bullied the younger boys in the College. We also watched DVDs; we particularly enjoyed *The Silence of the Lambs* and *The Hostel*. The latter production gave Flack some food for thought for Albert Noggins. It was to be Flack who gave me the idea. It was when we were settling down to watch *American History X*.

'Fancy a spliff sir', he asked with his usual air of informality.

'No I don't think so Wayne. I think the smell may be detected in the House. I don't think Mrs Read would appreciate the smell of burning cannabis wafting into her residence.'

Flack grinned before taking a gulp from his can of lager. 'Have a fag then.' He threw me a cigarette from across the room.

'No thanks but you carry on.'

'I had a little business to sort out with Selby today.' He was referring to George Selby, a Year 10 boy in Chamberlain.

'What business was that?'

'He owed me big time for protection money. Said he aint got none so I hit 'im.'

'Wayne you really must stop doing that.'

'But I thought you approved of that sort of thing, especially as 'e was one of the Chamberlain lot.' He looked confused.

'No, not that. You must stop using double negatives.'

'You what?' He looked even more confused.

'Never mind Wayne.' I smiled at him. There was something quite endearing about my young protégé.

Returning to his protection racket he said he had to curtail his punishment of Selby because Gloria Read had been approaching with a look in her eye that suggested Flack was in mortal danger. She didn't believe his story that Selby had been rude and informed Flack that her husband would hear of the incident.

'I 'ate that silly cow. Dunno 'ow the Doc puts up wiv 'er. If I was 'im I'd do 'er in, and if that didn't work I'd top me self.'

I suddenly became interested in his rantings. I now had an idea of how to get rid of Dr Dread.

When Flack left later in the evening I got to work on my lap-top.

Dear Dr Read,

I am a pupil at the School and I am in real trouble and I need to speak to you urgently. It really is a matter of life or death. Can you meet me on top of the Lion Yard car park on Tuesday 15th November at 7.00pm. Please do not speak to anyone else about this.

Tuesday 15th November was the very next day. My plan was to lure Read to the top of the three storey car park and push him over the edge. By seven o'clock it would be dark and the commuters would have left for home. I also was aware there were no CCTV cameras in that car park. I was also relying on the fact that he was a caring man and that he would certainly respond to this cry for help. In the meantime I would draft a suicide note from Read to say that he had taken his life because he couldn't bear to live with his dragon of a wife anymore.

During the lunch period on Tuesday I was in the process of completing the suicide note when there was a knock at the door. It was Flack; he wanted a lager from the fridge. I was preoccupied with the note and told him to help himself. He sat on the sofa watching some dreadful Australian soap opera. There was another knock at the door. This time it was Noggins asking for some pocket money. It was probably protection money for Flack. More than a little annoyed I went with Noggins to the House Study where the safe was located. The five pound note was handed over to the little worm and the entry made in the pocket money ledger. I returned to my flat to complete the note; Flack was still engrossed in his southern hemisphere escapism.

When everyone was at tea at six o'clock I drove the mile or so to the centre of Cambridge and made my way to the Lion Yard multi-storey car park. I parked my red Peugeot 207 on the second level; it was almost deserted. As I got out of the car I saw one of our cleaners put some shopping in the boot of her car. I got back into the car and hid my face until she had left the car park. When I was sure it was all clear I got out of the car again and walked the short distance to the stairs which led to Level 3. It was quite dark on the top floor although there were some dim security lights. I had to hope that when Read arrived there was no-one else on the top level. If that were the case the suicide would have to have been postponed. Also, I had to be quick as I couldn't afford to be caught in the act. It occurred to me that it was not going to be easy. The car park wall was over four feet high and Read was about fourteen or fifteen stone. I was anxious but utterly determined to carry it through. It wasn't cold for the time of year but it was raining steadily. I seemed to be there an age crouching beside a Toyota; it was too dark to determine the colour. Seven o'clock arrived and my heart began to race and I'm sure my mouth would have been dry had it not been for the falling rain. A car was approaching up the ramp from the second level.

5

It was not Read. Even as early as five past seven I was beginning to doubt that he would turn up as he was always so punctual. By quarter past seven I knew he would not be coming. I experienced mixed emotions of disappointment and relief. I waited until half past seven and then returned to the College.

When I got back to the College I noticed there was a couple of police cars parked outside the Headmaster's house. Although I was curious I went straight up to the boarding house study. Looking through the door window there was no sign of Read. Barry Clipper was on duty and busy marking while the boarders were engaged in prep. I did not disturb him and instead I returned to my flat. There I found Flack watching *EastEnders* with the usual can of lager in his hand. I must have looked despondent owing to the unsuccessful nature of the evening. Flack looked up at me.

'You've 'eard then?'

'Heard what?'

'About the doc.' He seemed surprised that I didn't know instantly what he was talking about.

'What about him?' Flack was mystified.

'He's bin done in.'

'What, killed?'

'Yeh, that's what I said.'

'Murdered?' Flack was becoming irritated by my inability to grasp the situation.

'Blimey, yes, murdered.' I stood there staring at Flack. He noticed that I had turned white. I was speechless, unable to fully take in what I had just heard.

'Well do we know who murdered him?'

'Dunno.' Flack continued to watch his tales about cockney life.

'Wayne, best you go back to your room. There could be a lot of activity in the House this evening, and I don't want anyone finding you here.'

'But there's only 'bout five minutes to go.' He was clearly not amused.

'Go on, scram!' Flack left my flat grunting. The Headmaster at some stage was probably going to become concerned about the House situation and come over to see how things were going.

I wondered who would have killed Read. I couldn't think of anyone on the staff; he was too popular. I thought that it could be a pupil, but failure to do prep was hardly a motive for doing away with your teacher. Mind you, I had been tempted to do just that to old Prossett, my Geography teacher, when I failed to hand in my work on glaciation. As the end credits of *EastEnders* appeared I was startled by the phone ringing. It was Lucy Dockett, the Headmaster's P.A. She informed me Grover-Smythe wanted to see me in his study immediately.

As I made my way through the corridors to the main College building it occurred to me that I didn't have an alibi for the time that Read was probably killed. Worse than this I wasn't where I would normally have been and that was in the staff dining room. My absence would have been noted; the same people attended each evening – the resident unmarried teachers and those on duty in the boarding houses. Every evening I had risked indigestion by having to listen to Peter Turner, our Physics teacher and a bachelor in his early fifties rabbit on about his numerous cruises. Only the previous evening we had to endure the entire voyage to South Georgia in the South Atlantic for the purpose of penguin spotting. When he wasn't boring us half to death with his maritime tales he would hum when eating his supper. Last Sunday, when chomping his way through roast beef and Yorkshire pudding he was also treating the rest of us to 'It's a long way to Tipperary'. Normally I would have told someone who was that irritating to take a running jump but I was obliged to tolerate the tales of Horatio Hornblower and his musical accompaniment because I had been informed that Peter Turner was the staff cricket team umpire. There was nothing worse in sport than a cricket umpire with a vendetta.

I knocked on the Headmaster's door believing I was about to be arrested for murder. As I entered his study the Headmaster was there with David Fotheringay, the Ferret, Lucy Dockett and a chap I didn't recognize. 'Ah Sebastian, please come in. Take a seat.' I made for the leather armchair next to the stranger. 'Sebastian, meet Detective Inspector Sugden.' Not a promising start, I thought, waiting for the handcuffs to be produced.

'Good evening Inspector', I said apprehensively. I didn't offer my hand fearing that the cuffs would immediately be shackled to my right wrist. I was sure everyone was aware of my nervousness.

'Evening sir.' He then turned to Grover-Smythe who was staring at me.

'Sebastian, you're probably aware of what has occurred here tonight?' I motioned to say something but the words just wouldn't come out. The Headmaster continued, 'It's dreadful, absolutely dreadful. Who could have done such a terrible thing?' I realized they didn't know who the murderer was. I began to relax a little. At that point Augustine Slabb, the Chaplain joined us.

'Come in Chaplain. We will need to discuss how we intend to tell the College.' Slabb responded to the Headmaster's point by suggesting that most of the College already knew. 'But how can that be?', asked the Headmaster in a way that suggested he was annoyed because someone had stolen his thunder.

'It might have something to do with the fact that Gloria Read was running around Hoare screaming that her husband had been murdered', responded the Chaplain.

Fotheringay asked how Read was murdered. The Head looked across to Detective Inspector Sugden. Sugden nodded as if to give permission to Grover-Smythe to answer his deputy's question.

'It appears it was poison administered with a hypodermic needle in all probability.' With the exception of the copper and Grover-Smythe everyone looked perplexed.

'Where did it happen?' It was the Ferret's turn to ask a question. The Head chose not to seek permission from the inspector before answering.

'Just outside the front door of Hoare. It hasn't been confirmed yet but he was killed some time between six thirty and seven o'clock', Sugden nodded again, 'Gloria last saw him at six thirty and Flack found him dead at seven.' I felt uncomfortable once more. I wondered why Flack hadn't told me that he was the one who had discovered Read. My deliberations were interrupted by being addressed by the Headmaster.

'Sebastian?'

'Headmaster?'

'I know this is a bit of an ask, and I appreciate you haven't been at the College long, but would you be prepared to take on Hoare on a temporary basis at least until we can find another housemaster?' He looked at me hopefully.

'Headmaster, in the circumstances of course I'll be prepared to step in. You can count on me.'

'Thank you Sebastian, I won't forget this.'

I had the impression that my presence was no longer required so I made my way to the door. My right hand grasped the brass door knob; at the same time Sugden asked the question I was dreading. 'For the record sir, can you tell me your movements between six thirty and seven o'clock? As I say just for the record.'

Still facing the door I closed my eyes and took a deep breath. By the time I turned around to face my inquisitor my answer was ready. 'I popped out to the supermarket to get a few items. I'm afraid no-one came with me.'

'And what time did you leave the School sir?'

'Oh about six o'clock I think.' I saw no reason to deviate from my time of departure for the Lion Yard car park.

'Out of interest what time did you return to School sir?'

'I was back by seven forty-five. I went straight to my flat in Hoare.'

'Ok sir, thanks very much. That will do for now.'

When I was the other side of the door I allowed myself a sigh of relief. It was short-lived however because I realized I had nothing to prove that I'd been to Sainsbury's. I also remembered that the suicide note I'd written on behalf of Read was still in the inside pocket of my jacket. Upon returning to my flat I placed it in the shredder. I then went to see Flack to tell him to call a house meeting. I didn't ask him about his grisly discovery earlier in the evening. In the meeting I confirmed that Read had died and that I was taking over as the housemaster. During the meeting many of the boys were in tears. Others just looked down in silence. Throughout the entire meeting Flack was grinning. I couldn't help but feel that in some way Flack was involved in Read's murder.

The police investigation continued over the next few days. A number of my colleagues were interviewed as were some pupils, including Flack. It would seem, at least according to the police, the murder weapon was a type of blow pipe or air gun. The poisoned dart had also been fired, or blown, at close range. The Police, and others including me were at a loss with regard to a likely motive. There appeared to be nobody, apart from me of course, who wanted Read out of the way.

24th November was Flack's birthday so I invited him into the flat for a snifter. As he was now eighteen I allowed him to have some champagne. Gloria Read was still resident in the Housemaster's House; she was given time to make the necessary arrangements before she left for the family home in the Lake District. I also presented Flack with a gift – a pair of olive green cords from Marks and Spencer. It was during our little coming of age soiree I received a visit from the Headmaster and Detective Inspector Sugden. The Headmaster was surprised to see Flack in my flat, and even more surprised to see a pair of olive green cords on his lap. Fortunately he was not in the process of trying them on. I explained to Grover-Smythe it was Flack's birthday although you could see by his expression that he was less than impressed with the idea that he was in my flat alone with me. Flack was asked to leave by the Headmaster. 'Sebastian, are you aware of any boys who were absent from the House the evening Donald Read was killed?'

I never had the faintest idea who was in the House and who wasn't but I made a credible effort to give it some consideration. 'Now let me see. No Headmaster, I believe everyone was in the House that evening. Why do you ask?' It was left to Sugden to answer my question.

'Mrs Read found a note in her late husband's briefcase. It suggests that Dr Read was on his way to meet with a pupil at seven o'clock on the evening he was killed.'

I attempted to look concerned in an ignorant sort of way. 'Well Inspector do you want to speak to the other housemasters to see if they can shed any light on the matter?', asked the Headmaster in a manner that suggested he was becoming bored with the investigation.

'Yes, if it's no trouble?'

'No trouble at all. Glad to be of assistance.'

'Thank you Sebastian. By the way we need to start looking for a replacement for Guy Straker. Perhaps we could discuss it at some stage tomorrow.'

Both men turned to leave but before Sugden got to the door he fired another question.

'Mr Punknowle?'

'Inspector?'

'Do you have a word processor in your flat?'

6

During the three weeks between Read's murder and the end of the Winter Term it appeared the Police had made no progress in apprehending the killer. Detectives led by Sugden continued to snoop around the campus but to no avail. No effort was ever made to inspect the contents of my food cupboard or my computer. In any event I had erased the suicide note just after drafting it so there was no chance of detection. By the end of term Gloria Read had departed taking her late husband's ashes with her to Windermere where she intended to scatter them over his beloved lake. However, I saw no point in moving into the Housemaster's residence until my permanent appointment was confirmed.

This period was also a very busy time for me. Although someone had disposed of Read for me I still had to consider my next move. I decided that the Ferret would be my main target for the Spring Term. However, before then I had other tasks to undertake. First of all I set in motion my plan to arrange a sixth form history trip to Washington DC during the Spring half term break. There was no intention to give the students an educational experience; I simply desired a free holiday and the opportunity to tread in the footsteps of Richard Nixon and Ronald Reagan. By the last day of term over twenty students had indicated an interest in the trip. For that group size I needed another member of staff. I therefore approached the Ferret who was delighted to accept my invitation. I think the nearest he had ever been to the USA was Lands End. But there was method in my madness and I saw in the trip to Washington an opportunity of addressing the Ferret issue. It was also getting closer to the January A-level modular examinations and it was important to my standing and reputation that my students performed well. The individual responsible for organizing examinations at the College was Theodore Clapp, the Examinations Officer. He kept all examination papers sent by the examination boards safely locked away in a cabinet in his office until the date of the examination. His office door was also locked. I had to find a way of getting into the filing cabinet to have a peek at the questions. I could then make sure my students had a decent chance of producing an excellent set of responses. The annual staff-versus-pupils hockey match presented me with a wonderful opportunity of achieving more than just a quick peek.

The evening before the match Flack was in his room in the process of handcuffing Noggins to a hot radiator. It was a typical Flack punishment for someone who had failed to obtain the *Playboy* magazine from the local newsagent. As Noggins was too young to purchase the adult publication he was expected to steal it. In any event his weekly allowance did not cover the cost of the magazine and Flack's protection money. I watched Flack's punishment session until Noggins started to weep.

'Wayne, can I have a word?' Flack snarled at his tormented victim.

'Hang on sir, I'll just let this miserable little git go.'

'Don't worry about that Wayne. I won't keep you long.' Noggins was sniveling as Flack followed me down the corridor and into my study. Barry Clipper was working at my desk as it was his duty evening. 'Get out Clipper. I need to talk to Wayne.'

'Yes of course Sebastian.'

'Mr Punknowle to you', said Flack with contempt as Clipper hurried out of the door. I was grateful to Flack for putting my junior colleague in his place.

'Wayne, I need you to do me a favour.'

'What's that then boss?'

'As you know tomorrow is the staff versus pupils hockey match and I need you to play.'

'You must be kiddin', I can't stand the stupid bloody game. Besides it's a girls' sport.' Clearly this was going to be more difficult than I first supposed. 'Hear me out first Wayne.' He gave me a look that suggested he would never comply with my request. 'I want you to play so you can take out Mr Clapp.' Flack began to look more at ease with the idea.

'What, you mean knobble 'im?'

'Yes, knobble him.' I was happy to adopt his rather basic terminology in an effort to win his support for the venture.

'I dunno boss. That bunch of creeps will never let me play. And I've my reputation to think about. I don't wanna be seen as some nancy boy who gets dressed up in girls' kit.'

'You don't need to wear a skirt Wayne.'

'But what about the others?' He was still not convinced.

'You can leave that to me; I'll make sure you are selected for the team.'

'Alright then, but apart from knobblin' old Clapp what else do I get out of it?' I placed my arm round his shoulder.

'Well my friend if you manage to break one of his legs or something I feel sure you will achieve some decent results in next term's exams.' Flack smirked his approval. Our little chat however was disturbed by Barry Clipper.

'Excuse me Mr Punknowle?'

'What is it now Clipper?'

'It's Albert, Albert Noggins. He appears to be attached to Flack's radiator.' Flack looked on in a way that suggested he was disinterested.

'Noggins seems to be suggesting that it was Flack who handcuffed him to the radiator', continued Clipper who was obviously intimidated by Flack's presence.

Trying to appear professional I asked Flack if he was aware of Noggins' predicament.

'Noggins is always cuffin' 'imself to me radiator sir. I think he's got a bit of a problem.'

'Damn attention seeker! Clipper I want Noggins to be put in House detention on Saturday morning. You can cover the session.' I was aware that every Saturday morning Clipper amused himself train spotting at Shelford railway station. Clipper appeared to be resigned to his fate.

'Wayne, would you mind releasing Noggins from your radiator?'

'No problem sir.'

'Oh and I'll see you at the match tomorrow.'

After breakfast the next morning I went directly to the Senior Common Room. Struggling to read the back page of the *Daily Telegraph* was Russ Dicker, the Director of Sport and affectionately known to the pupils as 'Big Dick.' Dicker was not a particularly bright member of staff, which of course was in keeping with most teachers of Physical Education. I was not surprised to learn that he achieved a third-class degree from the Bognor Regis Institute of Technology. He probably failed to obtain a second-class degree because of a dropped catch in the slips or he couldn't cope with bouncing and catching a tennis ball ten times in succession.

'Russ, just the man!' Still looking down at his newspaper he was obviously struggling with a word containing three syllables.

'Morning Seb. What can I do for you?' As I needed a favour I chose to ignore the over-familiar shortened version of my name. Also, I assumed he couldn't cope with my full first name.

'Would it be possible for Wayne Flack to play in the hockey match this afternoon?' He nearly spilt his coffee over some Geography coursework, which had been left on the table.

'You must be joking.' He looked at me as if I had just asked him for a loan of fifty thousand pounds.

'No I'm not joking. You see Wayne is keen to change his image. He appreciates that he is regarded as a rogue, but...'

'You can say that again.'

I ignored his rude interruption. As he was a soccer supporter I assumed he wasn't used to good manners. 'But he is very eager to change his ways and as his housemaster I would like to think we could give him a chance.'

'No way Seb. Besides the team has already been picked. I just can't drop one of the lads because that thug wants to play.' Clearly Russ had no concept of compassion. I was about to push Flack's case further when the phone rang. It was answered by Peter Turner. When he finished the call he came over to Dicker.

'Russ, that was Mrs Stubbs-Wilson. Dominic is unwell and will not be in School today. She said that he had information in the ear – an odd condition but there you are. She also mentioned that he will not therefore be able to play in the match this afternoon.'

I smiled at Dicker. 'You appear to be one short?' Dicker did not respond. 'Go on Russ give the lad a chance. You do this for me and I'll run one of your cricket teams in the summer term.' I was aware the College would be short of cricket team coaches. Dicker appeared interested in the proposition as it was always a mission to persuade colleagues to stand out in the warm sunshine in the afternoon.

'Ok he can play, but the first obscene word or jesture and he's off.'

'Oh absolutely old boy.'

'Well you just make sure he knows that. And tell him not to give the umpire any grief.'

'Leave it to me Russ. Thanks for this old man, I really do appreciate it.'

'I just hope I won't live to regret this.' I smiled knowing very well that only Clapp would regret Dicker's change of heart. I returned to Hoare where Flack was still in bed to give him the good news.

During my free periods that morning I managed to complete my end of term reports. I didn't know many of my pupils by name and more often than not I wrote reports on children I wasn't aware I taught. My mark book didn't help as there were no marks in it. There wasn't anything wrong with my record keeping. Indeed my records accurately reflected the situation; my mark book was devoid of marks simply because I hadn't marked anything. I decided upon a policy whereby everyone would receive a positive report. I believed that if the reports were positive it would satisfy the parental ego. At the various social occasions over the festive period parents would be able to boast about their child's excellent progress. They would also put this down, hopefully, to inspirational teaching. If, however, critical reports were sent out it would normally lead to parents questioning the quality of the teaching. As the Hoare House housemaster I was also responsible for writing reports on the boys in the House. I left Flack until last and of course I was determined to give him a glowing report.

Wayne has been an outstanding student throughout the term. It was not his fault that all his teachers seemed to have mislaid all the written work he handed in. I feel sure he will achieve some excellent results in the external examinations next term. As Head of House he has been a shining example to the other boys. He is a very compassionate young man who looks out especially for the young and vulnerable pupils in the House. Indeed he makes it his business to ensure that all the radiators are fully turned on thus ensuring the youngsters are not cold. He is always very well turned out and keeps his grade one haircut well groomed and his ear stud is always sparkling. I am hopeful that next term he will be appointed a College Prefect. Well done Wayne and keep up the good work.

The hockey team was surprised to see Flack in his College colours down at the astroturf. They were even more astonished to see me on the touch line. Like Flack I detested the game.

Dicker had instructed Flack to play at Right Back. His mission, however, was to 'mark' Clapp and therefore he annoyed Dicker and his team mates when he continued to play out of position. After twenty minutes of play Flack had not succeeded in making his attack upon the Examinations Officer. It was obvious that Dicker was becoming irritated by Flack's roaming and was considering replacing him with another player. Fortunately I was able to warn Flack about his impending substitution. Within seconds Flack launched himself like an Exocet missile into Clapp. The speed and ferocity of the impact caused Clapp to be thrown up in the air. He landed awkwardly with a tremendous thump. Flack was immediately dismissed from the field. I hung around, however, for the ambulance to arrive to take the poor Clapp to the Accident and Emergency department of Addenbrooke's Hospital.

The reports from the hospital were encouraging. Clapp had broken both legs and dislocated his shoulder and the Headmaster had been informed that he would not be back to College for at least ten weeks. He would miss the entire January examination session. The Headmaster was grateful to me for volunteering to step into the fray as the temporary Examination Officer while Clapp was recovering from Flack's brutal but brilliant assault. For the sake of appearances it was termed a sports injury and at my urging no action was taken against Flack.

And so the first term came to a satisfactory end. The murder of Read remained a mystery but I persuaded myself that it was a killing without motive and quite simply Read had been in the wrong place at the wrong time. My plans were working out very well; as housemaster I felt one step closer to the headship. By offering to take on examinations I had won the respect of the Headmaster and given myself the opportunity of achieving good academic results for my sixth form History students. The trip to Washington DC had been organised so I could look forward to dealing with the matter concerning the Ferret. On the last afternoon before we broke up I wished Flack well for the holiday and thanked him for his gallant efforts during the term. I also presented him with his Christmas gift – a pair of brown brogues and a book on the Kray twins. Following the College Carol Service in Cambridge Cathedral I left directly for Somerset where I was to spend the Christmas holiday with Uncle Rex and his family.

7

Uncle Rex had always described himself as a landowner. More accurately he owned a dairy farm that boasted one hundred acres, which was used for the grazing of one hundred and twenty Jersey cows. The farm was surrounded by some beautiful Somerset countryside with lovely views of the Quantock Hills. On a clear day it was possible to see the Wellington monument. The farm was about five miles to the south of Taunton just outside the tiny village of Mangersleigh. Although Uncle Rex owned the farm he did not work it; that was left to the farm manager, Walter Trull.

When I arrived at the farm the family was seated at their large pine table in the middle of the kitchen drinking hot chocolate. Uncle Rex was holding court in the company of his wife, my Aunt Mildred, and his son, my cousin Perkin. As usual Uncle Rex was smartly attired in a tweed suit. A tartan woollen tie went well with his red waistcoat and checked shirt. It was possible to see your reflection in the highly-polished brown shoes he had bought from *Russell & Bromley* twenty years previously. The gap between his waistcoat and the top of his trousers revealed a certain portliness. Uncle Rex was well into his sixties and although his grey hair was thinning on top he did support a large handlebar moustache. The moustache was a reminder of his time in the RAF. Contrary to his earlier lecture to my sixth form he had never in fact served in the Second World War. He had not even fired a shot in any war, nor had he ever been a pilot. He had completed his national service in the air force and with a little help from his father, who had some influence in the Air Ministry, managed to obtain a commission in the Supply Wing. Farming was not his first love, nor was Aunt Mildred come to that. His real passion was for classic cars and collecting Napoleonic porcelain figurines. He was particularly proud of his Imperial Guard infantry officer and a mounted trooper in the 15th Hussars.

Aunt Mildred was also into tweeds, and it would be unusual to not see her decked out in tweed skirt and jacket. When I arrived, however, she was wearing a green quilted jacket, which suggested she had just returned from walking the two golden retriever dogs. The fresh mud on the bottom of her boots supported the theory. Aunt Mildred was as pompous as her husband and there was certainly an air of authority about her. She regarded herself as lady of the manor and it was a brave vicar who did not consult Aunt Mildred on the content of his weekly sermon. She had been responsible for the removal of the previous parson; the Bishop of Bath and Wells had grown tired of her flow of letters complaining of the papist leanings of the Reverend Bungle. The Bishop believed it was in everyone's interest to have him moved to a parish near Bristol. She was certainly full of her own importance and everyone in the village took it for granted that she was in charge when it came to the summer fete and other local events, which included the village amateur dramatic society. If there was one weakness with Aunt Mildred it was the fact she was too indulgent of her son.

Cousin Perkin, in the way he dressed and in physical appearance, was the spitting image of his father. He had more hair and no moustache but in all other respects he was his father's son. However, although Perkin was about my age he did not have a job and both his parents seemed prepared to allow him to remain unemployed. He had tried to gain employment since he left his Land Management course at Cirencester College ten years previously but things didn't work out. For example he applied to become an army officer. Asked at interview why he wanted to join the army he replied that he preferred to wear green rather than air force blue or navy. However, he was always interested in military matters; even at his advanced age he was never happier than when playing with toy soldiers, forts and castles. On one of the kitchen work tops there was an *Airfix* model kit in the process of being painted and constructed. The box of the kit suggested that the finished article should look something like the German pocket battleship *Bismarck.* I understood that for Christmas he was hoping Santa Claus would bring him an *Action Man* frogman. Failing this he was rather expecting to find the *Captain Scarlet* Spectrum Patrol Vehicle among the usual pile of presents. Women had never interested Perkin and this suited Aunt Mildred who wanted her 'little soldier' never to leave home. There appeared to be no reason why Perkin would ever need to have a job. He received a handsome monthly allowance from his parents who he still referred to as 'mummy' and 'daddy' and of course one day he was to inherit the estate. Uncle Rex nearly disinherited him last week when Perkin chipped a porcelain Marshal Soult. He probably thought at the time that he was a gunner in the British artillery at Waterloo and projected a marble in the direction of the famous subordinate of the French emperor.

It occurred to me that if there was no Perkin I would be the one to inherit the farm. My financial situation had improved since getting the job at Lord Bilgebury but the repaying of numerous loans meant that my residual income was still rather limited. There was no way I could afford the type of trip Augustine Slabb was enjoying over the Christmas break. He had gone off to Australia on the first day of the holiday to take in the Ashes series. His intention was to attend the test matches in Adelaide, Melbourne and Sydney. In all he was to be in Australia for almost four weeks and it cost him a considerable amount of money. Russ Dicker thought it would have cost this latest recruit to the 'Barmy Army' something in the region of four thousand pounds. Mrs Slabb, who did not share her husband's love of cricket, did not travel with him; she was spending Christmas with her mother in Wrexham. Slabb was passionate about his cricket and no amount of cash or religious commitments was going to deny him the chance of seeing Australia versus England down under. Four weeks away from Mrs Slabb was also an undeniable bonus for a long suffering husband. I became very envious of the Chaplain especially as temperatures began to plummet and a hard frost became the daily norm. When we attended Midnight Mass on Christmas Eve the temperature was a chilling minus five degrees.

Christmas morning produced all that Perkin had hoped for. In addition to those items at the top of his list to Father Christmas there was a range of other items with which Perkin could occupy his time. He was particularly delighted with his new *Thunderbird 2*, especially so because the 'pod' contained a plastic *Thunderbird 4*. An excited Perkin also unwrapped a parcel that revealed a replica of the *Starship Enterprise* complete with miniatures of *Captain Kirk* and *Mr Spock*. Clearly Father Christmas had been pleased with the mince pie and glass of port left by Perkin the evening before. I caused Uncle Rex a little embarrassment when I handed Perkin a parcel containing an *Airfix* model kit of a Lancaster bomber. For my part I was entirely satisfied with my presents that Christmas. In addition to the numerous pairs of socks, Uncle Rex and Auntie Mildred were kind enough to give me a burgundy quilted smoking jacket.

After the Queen's message at three o'clock we sat down for a roast goose lunch. We were joined for our Christmas feast by my uncle's greatest friend, Colonel Humphrey Popplewell and his wife Agatha. There was an awkward silent pause when the Colonel asked if I was missing Picton College, my previous place of employ in Taunton before I was unfairly asked to leave following the house funds episode. Although Aunt Mildred was successful in quickly changing the subject to the nature of the Archbishop of Canterbury's Christmas address, I still felt a degree of anger for the shabby way I had been treated. While tucking into the sprouts I became lost in my own little world and paid no attention to the various conversations going on around the table. I desperately wanted revenge and began to contemplate ways of achieving satisfaction.

After the Christmas period the weather remained very cold and the hard frosts persisted. Not wishing to re-enact the Battle of Little Big Horn or some other military encounter with

Perkin I took myself off on long walks around the fields with the dogs. During one of these walks I received a text message from Wayne Flack.

Hello gov. how things goin. In bit of trouble. Bin chucked out of grandads house. No where 2 go. Can u put me up til get back 2 school. Wayne

It transpired that Flack had used a flick knife to cut the whiskers off his grandparents' cat and taking exception to this they had asked him to leave. He did not mention until later that he had boiled his grandmothers budgie in a saucepan because it was making too much noise during the Christmas edition of *EastEnders*.

I had reservations about Flack joining me in Somerset and having to explain things to Uncle Rex and Aunt Mildred, but there was no doubt that he would be quite useful. I persuaded my hosts that I wanted Flack to come down to the farm so I could help him with some revision. My sense of professionalism was applauded. I sent him a text.

Hi Wayne. Yes u may stay with me. I will meet u at Taunton railway station tonight at 8pm. Very important u wear cords and brogues. See you later. SP

Fortunately there was a small barn conversion next to the main house that was used for bed and breakfast guests. As there were no such guests staying over the holiday period Flack was allowed to stay there. By the time Flack arrived there was only a couple of days left of the holiday.

I think that two days was just about the limit as far as Aunt Mildred was concerned. To her Wayne was something quite alien and most disagreeable. From the very start of his short stay she was bemused by his version of the English spoken word and looked to me for translation. This was particularly the case when the term 'ponce' was used with reference to Perkin. Nor did she approve of the manner in which Wayne consumed champagne from her best cut crystal glass flutes. Rex had sometimes produced a mild hiccup, but the prolonged belching produced by Wayne was not appreciated. There was also an awkward situation when Wayne accompanied Aunt Mildred to procure some necessary comestibles at the local supermarket. Upon arriving home from the excursion, Aunt Mildred was somewhat perplexed as to how she had managed to acquire grocery and other items that didn't appear on the receipt. Never before in her life had she obtained cigarette filters from any form of retail establishment. For his part, Wayne did not exactly take to rural life. When attempting to communicate with a Jersey cow, the animal proceeded to project excrement on his new jeans and trainers. Uncle Rex kept out of Wayne's way for the most part however he couldn't understand how a chap could wear jewelry in his ear and confirmed his view of people who lived in urban areas.

On the last evening of our stay at the farm I decided to keep Wayne away from the family. Earlier he had kicked Perkin in the shin and *Thunderbird 2* had lost both wings and one of its engines. Aunt Mildred was more than happy to plate up some coq au vin so that Wayne and I could have our meal in the barn conversion. We pondered that evening how I could take my revenge on Picton College. It was not long before Flack came up with a plan. In the early hours of the morning we both left the farm and drove into Taunton.

Next morning I was awoken by the telephone in Uncle Rex's study. I put on my dressing gown and went downstairs.

I found Uncle Rex in the kitchen talking to Aunt Mildred. Perkin was at the table applying the nose cone to his *Saturn V* rocket. Uncle Rex looked in a state of high anxiety.

'Anything the matter?'

'Yes. I'm afraid so', replied my Aunt; Uncle Rex was still in a state of shock.

'What on earth has happened?' I sounded concerned. At last Uncle Rex contributed to the conversation.

'It's the School old boy. It's burned down.' Rarely had I seen him look so concerned.

'What all of it?' This was surely too much to hope for.

'Not exactly, but it's taken out the entire main building. School House, Dining Room, Kitchen, Head's study, Staff Room – all gone.'

As Chairman of Governors Uncle Rex was going to be extremely busy dealing with the consequences of the fire. I decided that I would return to Cambridge a day early and I went to wake Flack.

'Come on Wayne, time to get back to School'. As usual Flack was slow to respond and eleven o'clock was still very early for him.

'Why? What's goin' on?', he asked struggling to open his eyes.

'Nothing. We'll just be in the way if we stay around here.'

'There's not a problem is there?'

'No problem at all my friend. Just collect your stuff and we can be off. Don't forget to pick up those matches Wayne.' There was a box of *Swan* matches on his bedside cabinet. By one o'clock we were on the M5 making our way back to Cambridgeshire.

8

Upon my return to Lord Bilgebury I was invited to take up residence in the Housemaster's residence. I couldn't get out of the flat quickly enough; it was nothing more than a large box and fit only for Straker's replacement in the History Department, Robin Spilsby. Spilsby was aged twenty-two and a newly qualified teacher and certainly wasn't the best candidate for the job. But I didn't want the best candidate; I wanted someone who was going to do as they were told. I wasn't impressed with one candidate fresh from Durham University as he was far too much of an educationalist. I managed to persuade the Headmaster to drop any ideas about employing a pretty young thing from Cheshire. She was far too interested in social history and no doubt she would have brought her dreary tales of Knitting in Knutsford to Cambridge. Nor did I want someone who was going to outshine me in the classroom. Spilsby was perfect; he was of a nervous disposition and likely to struggle with classroom discipline. He wasn't one of those glamourous sporting types either; they tended to be far too popular for my liking. Yes, Spilsby could be intimidated in the same way I intimidated Harold Pryke, and I could continue to reign supreme in the History Department.

It didn't take the estate department very long to move my furniture and other belongings across to my new abode; the process was completed in only twenty minutes and that included a break for tea and chocolate digestive biscuits. In addition to having three bedrooms my new residence had a large sitting room, dining room and a decent size kitchen. I felt like Adolf Hitler arriving at his new Chancellery for the first time. The residence had the added bonus of being detached from the boarding house. No more would there be the smell of unwashed socks and oriental cooking.

The return of the boarders in January for the start of the Spring Term was something of a chore. In addition to the usual invitations to dinner and reports of holidays spent in far-away climes there were also a number of difficult parental enquiries to negotiate. At least two mothers enquired as to the whereabouts of Mrs Punknowle. As I assumed they were not referring to my mother I had to explain that I was not married. I could detect their concern from the expression on their faces; it was a look that suggested they were certain I had homosexual tendencies and that a day school would be a better place for their offspring.

I had to endure a tricky few minutes with Mrs Noggins, the mother of Albert. I imagined her, bearing in mind the nature of her son, to be a timid and unassuming female. Nothing could be further from the truth. Indeed she exhibited all the traits of a crocodile. I was particularly unnerved by the bulging eyes and continuous snapping of the mouth. Indeed Nancy Noggins, I later discovered, had something of a reputation as a battleaxe who regularly berated prep school teachers for not doing their best for her children. Albert was the eldest of five children. This odious woman had the nerve to suggest that I had turned a blind eye to her son being bullied by Flack. The crocodile snapped at me relentlessly and left me in no doubt that if Albert continued to be victimized she would raise the matter with the Headmaster. Like some of the other parents she also made the point that she was surprised the Headmaster had allowed a bachelor to take over the running of the boarding house. Clearly the crocodile did not like me and this was a real concern as I learned that her lawyer husband was in line to become a member of the College Board of Governors. I gained two things from the crocodile experience. Firstly I had to ensure Flack stopped tormenting Noggins, and secondly it became apparent that if I wanted to become the Headmaster of Lord Bilgebury College I would have to marry – and quickly.

For the time being, however, matrimony would have to wait as there were other matters in need of my urgent attention in the first week of the new term. I had to prepare for the Washington trip but the most pressing item on the agenda was the public examinations that were to start on the first Monday of term. On the Saturday I had gone into town to have two new keys cut. One key was for the Exam Office and the other was for the cupboard where the examination papers were stored before they were attempted by the pupils.

All the papers had arrived for the January session by the previous Friday and I stored them in the locked cupboard in the order in which they were to be taken. Physical Education Paper One was to be sat on the Monday morning. The first History paper was to be taken on Tuesday afternoon in the second week of term.

Following the PE exam on the Monday I collected the papers and went back to the Examination Office to make the necessary arrangement for their dispatch to the person responsible for the marking of a script – probably to someone who had no idea about bio-mechanics or the psychology of sport or how to assess the responses. It would also appear that Dicker's candidates had little idea either. I understand there are in fact insufficient people who are prepared to be examiners. This is hardly surprising when marking has to be the worst job in education and this is compounded by the fact that examiners receive a meagre one pound ninety-five for every script they mark. It is a known fact that examination boards have to employ 'rogue' examiners to mark papers owing to a shortfall in people who might actually know something about the subject. I understand the tea lady at the Cambridge Examining Group was required to mark four hundred scripts in the previous summer's GCSE Biology exam.

Having sealed the PE responses in an envelope to be sent to a Mr Snootwell on the Isle of Wight I extracted the History paper that was to be attempted in just over a week's time. I knew that to open the packet would entail considerable risk. An examination board inspector could turn up at any time and request to inspect the cupboard. If discovered I knew I would most certainly be dismissed from the College and probably barred from teaching ever again. I deemed the risk worth the taking. Carefully, with a pair of scissors, I slit open the plastic packaging. Before proceeding to examine the contents I made sure my office door was locked. Satisfied that there was no danger of an untimely interruption I calmly extracted an exam paper.

It had been worth the risk. The History candidates were to be given a choice of three questions and they were required to answer two. They would have been unable to attempt any of the three questions. This was not a reflection upon their ability; I had not managed to teach them the content. Obviously I had concentrated my efforts on the beneficial aspects of Hitler's rule in Germany and I had spent half the previous term looking at Stalin and the reasons for his greatness. I was therefore a little irritated to discover questions concerning the reasons for Germany's defeat in the Second World War and Stalin's crimes in the period 1924 to 1953. The third question concerned Woodrow Wilson and I hadn't bothered with him at all. Although not on the syllabus I had also spent some time looking at the masterful presidency of George W. Bush. In my opinion the examiners who had chosen the questions had been very narrow-minded and promoted an ultra liberal bias. I replaced the opened packet right at the back of the cupboard and proceeded to open the packets containing the French and English exam papers. I did not bother to have a look at the questions and both packets joined History at the back of the cupboard.

After locking the cupboard and the office door I made my way to the Staff Room to find it devoid of any colleagues. It was lunch time and very probably they were stuffing themselves with Angelica Smite's stew and dumplings and spotted dick. Every member of the teaching staff had a pigeon hole for mail. The more efficient teachers tended to empty their pigeon holes every day and even I managed to bin the contents at least once a week. There were colleagues, however, who rarely removed any items for several weeks. The pigeon hole directly to the right of mine was a classic example of this type of hoarding. It was into this pigeon hole that I placed two items to the rear of the unread letters and memos, dust laden text books, a moth eaten scarf and at least one apple core. My task now was to inform my students of my findings without rousing suspicion.

For some reason my History students were a little concerned when I gave them my question 'predictions' the following morning. One arrogant lout had the cheek to suggest my teaching had lacked a certain thoroughness. I reminded the ungrateful dim wit and his class mates that Advanced level was all about independent learning and that clearly he and the others had not done enough of it. As far as I was concerned it was job done and time to consider other items on the Punknowle agenda.

We were due to go on the Washington trip during the February half term break. Twenty five boys had signed up for the trip, including Wayne Flack, and the payment to the travel company, Dodo Tours, was due. The cost of the trip was six hundred and fifty pounds per student. However, I charged them seven hundred and fifty pounds and cheques were to be made payable to me. After all I had my meals and champagne to consider whilst on the trip. Also I was in need of a new stereo system. Owing to the cat and budgie saga, Wayne's grandfather had refused to pay for the trip and therefore this was another consideration in the costings. In addition to the Ferret I also asked the Chaplain to join us on the trip. The thought of the Ferret warbling on at me about educational initiatives in the *Hawk & Dove* restaurant where the great Richard Nixon once ate Maryland crab cakes filled me with dread. At least I would have the Chaplain with which to chew over the cud with regard to recent England cricket performances. It was also vitally important to have Slabb on side if I was to make a successful bid for the headship. Certainly he was delighted to receive my invitation and accepted without delay. I knew the Ferret was a photography enthusiast and he was happy to act as the official trip photographer.

Following morning assembly on the Friday of the first week of term I received a call from Anita Jugg, the College Secretary. I went somewhat weak at the knees when she relayed to me that the Examination Board Inspector had arrived and was waiting for me at Reception. Not wishing to create the impression that I was hiding anything I made my way with some haste to greet my visitor. With thinning grey hair he looked the very image of a retired Gestapo officer. Wearing a long black mack he was no more than about five feet tall. Peering at me over his rimless spectacles he made no effort to offer me his hand in greeting. Wishing to get off to a good start I offered my own hand. Taken aback by this gesture he removed the black leather glove from his right hand and limply took my hand. It was left to me to start the up and down motion of the hand shake routine.

'Good morning. Sebastian Punknowle, the Exams Officer.'

'Bimley.'

'Pardon?' I asked not really understanding what he was talking about.

'Arthur Bimley from the Board.'

'Yes of course. Can I offer you a cup of coffee?' I remember trying this before!

'No thank you. Can we make our way to the exam hall please?'

On our way to the Sports Hall it was obvious that he wasn't willing to engage in any sort of pleasant communication such as the weather or the recent Ashes tour down under.

The Ferret had started off the Geography exam and fortunately everything appeared to be in order upon our arrival in the hall. Bimley then proceeded to walk up and down the aisles between the exam desks. Occasionally he took out a tape measure to work out the distance between each desk. After one such measurement he removed a little black book from the inside chest pocket of his mack to make a note with a black *bic* pen. After checking the paperwork on the front desk where we conducted the administration of the exams he indicated that he wished to leave the hall.

'One point three meters', he announced with a degree of smugness.

'I'm sorry, what…?'

Without being permitted to finish asking what on earth he was talking about he informed me that the distances between some desks were not the regulation distance of one point five meters. Somewhat irritated I enquired as to whether he was perhaps being a little on the fussy side. This was a mistake. 'Mr Punknowle, regulations are regulations and you are in breach of Board Regulation 46, section B, part 2. Furthermore, at least one of the candidates was using a blue pen when

Regulation 98 clearly states that black pens are to be employed by the examination candidates.'

Although making another mistake I couldn't help myself, 'As a matter of interest Mr Bimley what is Regulation 99?'

Clearly annoyed by the sarcastic nature of my question he informed me he wanted to inspect the Examination Office.

'Where are the examination papers kept Mr Punknowle?', he asked with the black book at the ready.

'In that large cupboard in the corner.' He peered over his spectacles before asking the predictable question.

'Is it kept locked?'

'Yes of course', I responded matter-of-factly.

'And who has a key to this office and the cupboard?' I felt his Gestapo senses were leading him to a place I didn't want him to go.

'I have one set and there is another set in the Headmaster's Study.' I made no reference to the keys I had cut the previous week.

'May I inspect the contents of the cupboard?' At this point I realized that Plan B would have to be put into operation. I opened the cupboard and stood back to allow him to have his rummage. It did not take him long, 'The English, History and French papers appear to be missing Mr Punknowle!'

Appearing shocked I declared that was impossible and proceeded to do my own bit of rummaging. 'Good grief, I don't believe it. How could this have happened?' I hoped my sense of anxiety appeared plausible. The opened examination paper envelopes were where I had placed them – at the back of the cupboard.

'This is a very serious matter Mr Punknowle. The entire examination system in this school has been compromised.'

'I just don't understand how this could have happened.'

'Mr Punknowle, I will need to speak to the Head right away.'

'Yes of course, Mr Bimley.'

Grover-Smyth was outraged when Bimley made his report. 'Sebastian, how on earth could this breach of security have occurred?'

'I really have no idea sir.'

'Well who has a key to your office?'

'Obviously I have a key and you have one as well.'

'Me!' Lucy Dockett confirmed the arrangement.

Time for Plan B. 'I wonder?'

'What is it? What do you wonder?', demanded Grover-Smyth.

'The exam packets that have been opened.'

'What about them Sebastian?'

'Well. No it's not possible.'

'For goodness sake Sebastian tell us what you're thinking.'

It's probably nothing Headmaster but it occurs to me that David Mingford takes all three subjects.'

'Surely you don't think that Bob Mingford has anything to do with this?', retorted Grover-Smyth.

'Of course not Headmaster, Bob is beyond reproach. I know he would do anything for David but I'm sure he wouldn't cheat.'

'Bob Mingford?', asked Bimley, black book at the ready.

Grover-Smyth responded that Bob Mingford was Head of Music; his son David was in the sixth form. 'David has received a conditional place to read English Literature at Oxford. There's absolutely no way that Bob is a cheat', proclaimed Grover-Smyth with a degree of apprehension. He knew he couldn't afford to lose both his Head of Music and Lord Bilgebury College's only realistic Oxbridge candidate for this year.

The Gestapo man, however, refused to let go. 'Nonetheless Headmaster the matter requires investigation.'

Grover-Smyth was left with no alternative but to ask Bob Mingford to come up to his study. Mingford was shocked and very angry when he learned of the reasons for his summons. On at least two occasions during his Gestapo interrogation he glanced across at me. I in turn looked toward Grover-Smyth who was still convinced Mingford was innocent of any wrong doing. He was unsure as to how to proceed and looked to me for help. 'Bob is clearly innocent Sebastian. What do you suggest?'

'Of course Bob has done nothing wrong.' Looking over to Mingford I asked him to produce his set of keys. 'As I thought no keys to the Exam Office here', I assured the Head and Gestapo. The Gestapo, thankfully, was not convinced.

Peering once again over his spectacles Bimley turned toward Mingford. 'Do you have a desk or locker in the School, Mr Mingford?'

'Yes, I have both.'

'Then you will not mind if we check the contents?', enquired the astute Bimley. No-one detected my slight smirk.

'Please go ahead. I have nothing to hide.'

We all made our way to his classroom where Mingford emptied the contents of his desk drawers. Grover-Smyth looked relieved, 'Is there any need to continue with this ridiculous line of enquiry?'

Bimley appeared to ignore Grover-Smyth's comments. 'And where will we find your locker Mr Mingford?'

We all entered the staff room where a number of colleagues were present. It was obvious we had disturbed an in-depth conversation, possibly on recent educational reforms, but very probably not. Mingford emptied his crammed full pigeon hole placing the contents on a table to the side of the pigeon holes. The apple core, however, was thrown into waste paper basket. Before very long Mingford reached the rear of his pigeon hole. 'I don't believe it!' Mingford turned towards us and presented the keys to the Exams Office and the cupboard.

It proved impossible for Mingford to defend himself. At the age of fifty-six he was permitted to take early retirement rather than be sacked. No student was allowed to sit the History, English or French exams at the College. Bimley and the Board accepted that this was an isolated incident and the College was allowed to continue to operate as an examination centre. My History students were not able to benefit from my little peek but no blame was attached to me. I had liked Bob Mingford but Plan B was necessary if I was to survive Bimley's investigation.

9

I have always found January to be a dreary month as it doesn't actually lead anywhere apart from February, which can be equally dull and uninspiring. It was during this atmosphere of gloom and despondency that I contemplated a project to relieve the tedium. During one of my winter walks in Somerset over the Christmas holiday I thought about writing a book. The purpose of the book would be not only to raise money for the Punknowle coffers, but also to address some historical myths. Questions such as did Hitler really intend on invading Britain in 1940 was one theme for possible investigation. Another idea was to look at the abdication crisis of 1936. History books have led us to believe that Edward VIII had to give up the throne in order to marry Mrs Wallis Simpson.

However, I am of the belief that Mrs Simpson was an excuse for the establishment to be rid of Edward VIII. The government of the day certainly didn't approve of his views on foreign policy and his perceived admiration of Adolf Hitler. Nor did the government appreciate his meddling in domestic politics by his support for the working classes during the depression. Cosmo Lang, the Archbishop of Canterbury, resented the fact that he no longer enjoyed a close relationship with the Sovereign. King George V had regarded the Archbishop as very much part of the family. The King's advisors regarded Edward VIII as a danger to the monarchy because they believed he did not take his job seriously, went on long holidays and left wine stains on official government papers. Fortunately for all the opponents of the King, there was Mrs Simpson to ensure that Edward VIII would be forced to abdicate in favour of the more agreeable brother, George VI, the former Duke of York.

Thus far in the new year there had been no heavy snow to close the College down for a few days. A substantial downfall last winter in Taunton created sufficient chaos to extend the Christmas holiday by four days. No such luck in Cambridge. Of course there was always Washington to look forward to, especially the planned demise of the Ferret, but that was still some time away. To make matters worse I had received an invitation to attend the Lord Bilgebury College Burns Supper on the last Friday of the month. The organisers of this ghastly Scottish nationalistic ceremony were Angus and Megan Longmuir. Formerly of the city of Glasgow the couple had sought asylum in England twenty years previously in an effort to escape the mosquitos of Loch Lomond and to experience a cricket season that lasted longer than two weeks – the approximate length of a Scottish summer.

When sober, Angus taught English. At best his pupils found his accent difficult to understand. The daily half bottle of Glenbarry whisky before morning break would normally make the task of comprehension almost impossible and produce an excellent impression of an Afghan goat herder who had recently been hit by a wayward golf ball in the region of the Trossachs.

Meggie, his wife of over thirty years, was certainly not a teacher as her qualifications extended to an O Level in Home

Economics. Her primary task was to arrange social events during the course of the College year. There could be no doubting, however, that the highlight of the social calendar, as far as the Longmuirs were concerned, was the forthcoming bash to celebrate the life of Robert Burns. Her last effort to entertain the Lord Bilgebury College inmates was during the previous summer term and was considered a tremendous success by all who attended. According to Fotheringay the food was superb, the table arrangements were stunning and the guest speaker was thoroughly entertaining. However, nobody was quite able to work out the link between the theme for the dinner, the anniversary of Waterloo, and the décor – pictures and other paraphernalia associated with the history of steam railways. It would appear that dearest Meggie had been confused over the location of Wellington's famous victory in 1815.

On the evening of the dinner I was seated between Augustine Slabb and his wife Miranda. Mrs Slabb was the power in the Slabb abode, Primrose Cottage, situated on the edge of the south side of the College campus. Augustine did exactly what he was told and this extended to matters concerning religion. Miranda, a teetotaller, was raised in North Wales where English is spoken on occasions with a degree of reluctance. Her late father had been a fiery minister of the Presbyterian Church of Wales in the parish of Holywell, and his daughter had inherited his extreme sense of morality. Fun was never a notion considered in Primrose Cottage and certainly alcohol was never to be seen in the den of morality. Augustine has been known to have the odd drop of sherry at the staff bar, but Miranda was never made aware of such lapses in moral fortitude. An invitation to a Slabb dinner party was something to be avoided. Apparently it was not unlike attending a protestant version of the Inquisition.

Other members of the table included two sets of parents, Mr and Mrs Duncley and Mr and Mrs Rutt. Apparently I taught their children, but the names were unfamiliar to me. We were joined by Peter Turner who was already humming *Flower of Scotland*, having just bored Mrs Rutt with a report of his latest voyage of discovery around the Baltic. Mrs Rutt had been a little surprised to have ascertained that the purpose of the trip had been to procure decorations for his Christmas tree. To ensure a gender balance to the table Lucy Dockett, the Head's PA, was seated to the right of the Reverend Slabb. Miranda Slabb, with regularity, glared at Miss Dockett with contempt, especially when Lucy took it upon herself to remove a morsel of haggis from the lapel of Augustine's dinner jacket, which had managed to ricochet away from the edge of his mouth.

The dubious honour of celebrating the immortal memory of Scotland's national poet had fallen to the Headmaster. Grover-Smyth was in his element; he like most headmasters enjoyed being the centre of attention. It helped, of course, that most of his audience were already under the influence of a mixture of inexpensive Chilean wine and even cheaper whisky. They were induced to laugh at parts of the speech that had not been intended to be funny. Grover-Smyth was gratified, although a little bemused.

Lucy Dockett was in a state of trance, looking admiringly upon our leader. I was reminded of Adolf Hitler; he had the same effect on young women in the 1930s. I had showed my

Year 11 class a clip of a Hitler rally in Nuremberg in 1937. Cheering in the crowd was a girl who was not dissimilar in appearance to a young looking Margaret Thatcher. Miranda continued to glare. Grover-Smyth rambled on in the mistaken belief that his audience was enjoying his oration tracking the career of the Bard of Scotland. After about thirty minutes those assembled at the Longmuir highland gathering began to tire of laughter and applause and were somewhat relieved that Burns had died when he was only thirty seven. When the Headmaster eventually finished his biography with tales of Nelly Kilpatrick, among others, there was muted applause. Miss Dockett was alone in giving Grover-Smyth a standing ovation. Mrs Rutt prodded Mr Rutt in an effort to arouse him out of a temporary snooze. Not realising the speech was over, Mr Rutt proceeded to applaud. I noticed that Augustine Slabb had not been clapping. Indeed there was a look of scorn in the way that Slabb continued to stare at the Headmaster, even when Grover-Smyth took his seat with an air of deluded satisfaction. Lucy Dockett, however, continued to beam. 'Isn't he wonderful!', she pronounced with pride.

'I don't think so', retorted Slabb quietly. The nature of the response was entirely out of character.

'You alright Slabby?', I enquired with some mystification. The Miranda glare had rotated from Lucy to her husband.

'Yes, quite alright thank you', came the unconvincing reply.

By now the two sets of parents had left the table to bore someone else in the dining hall. Peter Turner was quietly humming *Loch Lomond.* He seemed happy to people watch and took no interest in the deliberations of his fellow table quests. I persevered with Slabb. 'Come on Slabby. What's up old man?'

Not for the first time in their marriage, Miranda spoke for him. 'He's sulking.'

'Sulking', I enquired, 'Sulking over what?'

'The cricket pavilion. He's upset because a new one isn't being built. It's pathetic', snorted Miranda. 'If he had as much interest in the Church as he did in that silly game he would probably be Archbishop of Canterbury by now.'

With both hands stretched out in front of him firmly gripping the table, Slabb responded to his wife's less than gracious remarks. 'It's not just about the pavilion, it's about the whole future of cricket at the College.'

'What do you mean Slabby?' I was becoming a little concerned for I too loved the great game.

The Chaplain drew breath and then proceeded to respond to my enquiry. 'It would seem the Headmaster means to get rid of cricket at Bilgebury in the next academic year.'

'Good grief, surely he wouldn't do that?'

'I am afraid dear boy he has already made the decision.'

The gravity of Slabb's announcement astounded me. 'But why Slabby?'

'Loathsome economics.'

I did not grasp the meaning of his line of response. 'You what?'

Still clasping the off-white table cloth he informed me that Grover-Smyth wanted to introduce girls into Lord Bilgebury College. He believed that in order to attract females it would be necessary to have sporting activities in the summer in which girls could participate. The Headmaster had also made the point that cricket got in the way of exam preparation.

I could not believe my ears. The prospect of having girls at Lord Bilgebury College filled me with dread. Not only would there be the inevitable pregnancies, we would also have to endure games like rounders and lacrosse. Worse than this, netball would be introduced to be played by females bearing names such as Brenda and Janet.

'This is absolutely ghastly. Is this true Lucy?'

The Headmaster's PA shuffled uncomfortably, refusing to respond to my probing. It was if she was trying to avoid emitting gas in polite company.

'Silence is consent then?'

With the exception of Peter Turner, who was still humming, all the others around the table joined Miranda Slabb in glaring at Lucy Dockett. Claiming the need for a visit to the ladies room she collected her hand-bag from the table and with haste made her way to the door. Entirely focussed on the escape route in front of her, she failed to see the bagpipes on the floor next to where the piper was downing yet another glass of cheap whisky. Grabbing hold of the piper's kilt in a vain attempt to break her fall she managed only to remove the tartan garment from the man's waist. The sporran landed on Lucy's head. Although the piper was too heavily under the influence to notice his de-frocking, there was a momentary hush around the dining room as Lucy Dockett attempted to recover from her fall from grace. Chatter was restored only when the Headmaster strode purposefully to the rescue of his downed PA.

Having decided the evening was about to descend into immorality, Miranda took her husband by the wrist and led him to the safety of Primrose Cottage. Only Peter Turner and I were left on the table.

'I didn't like the sound of what Augustine was saying.' Peter Turner had been listening after all.

'No, all very worrying.'

'I will miss my umpiring Sebastian.' From what I had heard the First XI coach and players would not necessarily share his sentiments.

'Well I was hoping to look after the Second XI.' I had pencilled in Wayne Flack to be my captain.

'I intend to address the matter with the Headmaster. We must not allow that red brick upstart to get rid of an English tradition at Bilgebury.' This was fighting talk from Peter Turner. 'Of course it's all Donald Read's fault.'

'I'm sorry Peter?' I was taken aback by this lack of respect for one who had only recently departed this mortal coil.

'Read was the one who persuaded the Headmaster to get rid of cricket at the School. I overheard both of them discussing it just prior to the Autumn half term. I have to say I was so bloody angry.'

I had never seen Peter Turner so animated, not even when he was recalling one of his adventures upon the high seas. Walking back alone to Hoare House it did occur to me that Peter Turner could have had something to do with Donald Read's murder. You read about it all the time: lonely men at home thinking about killing people. Certainly he had a motive; his love of cricket was not in doubt. It seemed he revelled in the power associated with the raised index finger. He also had opportunity. His flat was located next to Hoare House. From his window he could have seen Donald Read leaving or approaching the boarding house. The deadly dart could have been projected from the same window from some form of air gun.

I would employ Flack to investigate the contents of Peter Turner's flat.

10

Flack had not been able to find a single piece of evidence linking Peter Turner with the murder of Donald Read. It came as something of a surprise, however, that Turner wore *Hugo Boss* underwear. I was not convinced that Flack had been too thorough in carrying out the snooping operation but in any event I did not suppose that Turner would leave a gun, poisonous dart or any other incriminating item lying around his flat; not even under several pairs of *Hugo Boss* underpants.

February half term and the Washington DC trip were fast approaching and I had been putting the final touches to the itinerary. Wayne was confused as to why the Library of Congress was on the schedule. Wayne did not visit libraries because they tended to be linked to scholastic endeavour. For the same reason he missed lessons on a regular basis.

On the Wednesday evening before the weekend we were to leave for Washington, Wayne was in my residence watching one of those dreadful reality TV productions. From what I could make out some male sporting celebrity had the task of selecting a dinner date from a range of uneducated females. Every so often blonde tarts, from a selection of urban conurbations somewhere just south of Hadrian's Wall, had the acute embarrassment of being informed they were not worthy to share a slap up five course dinner in an exclusive restaurant on the King's Road with a recently retired Premiership footballer.

Later on in the evening, just after a bimbo from Halifax had been dispatched from reality to the real world of the minimum wage existence of the Hester supermarket chain, I received a potentially life-changing phone call. Upon the advice of Uncle Rex, the Chairman of the Cambridge Conservative Association, Bertram Prior-Astby, enquired as to whether I would be interested in becoming a candidate in the forthcoming District Council elections in May. Quite by chance Uncle Rex had come across Bertram Prior-Astby at a Classic Cars Appreciation Society rally at Goodwood in Sussex the previous weekend. The Chairman of the Association had indicated to Uncle Rex that the Tories were rather short of candidates and Uncle Rex had mentioned me as a possibility.

Without considering the consequences I immediately replied to the telephone enquiry in the affirmative. I thought this could be the start of a glittering political career. I had visions of waving to enthusiastic well-wishers on the steps of 10 Downing Street having won a landslide general election victory. I would not need to bother with the headship of Lord Bilgebury College. The prospect of becoming Prime Minister and achieving greatness beckoned. The District Council election was to represent only the beginning of my walk with destiny. I was duly invited to contest the Crankton ward, a large village three miles to the south of Cambridge.

However, the start of my political career would have to wait for a few days; the trip to Washington DC was imminent.

11

The first day of the half term and we are on our way to Heathrow courtesy of the Pitt Travel Coach Company. There are twenty eight of us in all: twenty five sixth formers, the Ferret, Augustine Slabb and my good self, the group leader. We are to be met by the tour company representative at the airport. Within half an hour of leaving Lord Bilgebury College at the unsociable hour of five o'clock in the morning, the Chaplain had dozed off leaving me to endure the bleatings of the Ferret. He was meandering on about some new academic monitoring initiative.

'Give it a rest Tim, it's only five-thirty, and anyway we're supposed to be on holiday.'

'Hardly a holiday Sebastian. Remember, we are responsible for a significant number of pupils going to a foreign land.'

'We're not exactly going to Tehran.'

'Yes, I know, but America can be a dangerous place. Certainly Washington is infamous for the number of murders.'

'They call them homicides over there.'

'Whatever they call them, Washington is still a dangerous place. And as the senior member of staff on this trip I must insist we keep a close eye on the boys.'

'Well Slabby seems to be failing in that respect.' The Ferret looked across to the Chaplain. His head leaning against the window, he had his arms folded across his chest. Although wearing his trusted grey herringbone jacket with curling lapels, there was no sign of the dog collar or black clerical shirt. Underneath his jacket he was wearing some form of multi-coloured garment that could have very easily been purchased at a beach shop in Hawaii. The Ferret, who was more sensibly attired in various articles obtained from Marks and Spencer, sighed as he observed Augustine Slabb dribbling slightly from the left side of his mouth.

'You have more of that to come old bean.' I motioned with my right index finger to the advance of Slabb's dribble. A droplet had just landed upon a palm tree leaf located just below the collar of his Hawaiian shirt.

'What on earth do you mean Sebastian?' It was at this point I took immense satisfaction in informing the Ferret that he was to share a hotel room with the Reverend. With another sigh he remarked that he hoped Slabb did not snore.

'There's more than his snoring to worry about Tim old boy.' I was enjoying this.

'Oh Lord! He doesn't talk in his sleep does he?'

'Don't know about that, but I would suggest that your main problem may well be fidgeting and bed socks.'

'What on earth are you talking about?'

At this point I delivered my bombshell. 'Unfortunately our hotel doesn't have any twin rooms. I'm afraid they're all doubles, which means you're going to have to share with Augustine.'

Clearly the Ferret was unimpressed with the sleeping arrangements. 'Why on earth could you not have put us in single rooms?

'Cost old boy. Unfair to make the parents pay for the comfort of the teachers on the trip.'

'What about you? Where are you sleeping?'

'In the hotel annex. They have a modest suite of rooms there.'

The Ferret continued to mutter and complain all the way to the airport. However, there was no way I was going to alter the arrangements and he would just have to put up with sharing a bed with Slabb. It was my sincere hope, however, that all would be well and that Slabb's presence in the bed would wreck any idea of the unfortunate Ferret having a good night's sleep!

Upon our arrival at Heathrow we had to endure the usual and tedious checking-in procedure. One did one's best to avoid any contact with *Easyjet* passengers for fear of catching something unpleasant. It was evident, however, that the family in front of me waiting to be scanned were off to some awful place such as Ibiza or Benidorm and had chosen the low cost, low-lifes mode of transport to get them there. The leader of the family, with a probable staple diet of crisps and lager, was wearing his holiday kit of off-white t-shirt, union jack shorts and cheap black trainers. If this wasn't enough, he was also wearing black socks. He left the supervision of their six noisy and demanding children to his obviously long suffering wife.

There was a major issue as Slabb made his way through the security scanner. Having been obliged to remove his belt he proceeded to lose his trousers and thus revealed a very fetching pair of blue boxer shorts and garters. The Ferret was obviously embarrassed by the scene that had unravelled before him, but like our students I found the entire experience extremely amusing. Once the Chaplain had collected himself, the group made their way *en masse* to the departure area to await our flight to the United States.

Apparently there had been no issues on the flight to Washington. Anyway I would not have been aware of any problems as I was enjoying a decent meal and well-deserved nap in Business Class. I left the supervision of the tour party to the Ferret and Slabb in the squalor of the economy cattle class section of the *British Airways* Jumbo Jet.

After the eight-hour flight I was feeling reasonably fresh as we touched down at Washington Dulles Airport at about one o'clock in the afternoon local time. With a five hour time difference I calculated it was six o'clock in the evening in Cambridge. Having made this trip previously I appreciated the need to stay awake until at least ten o'clock in order to avoid the adverse effects of jet lag. As we alighted the plane I noticed the Ferret was looking a little worse for wear and therefore I recommended he take a nap when we reached the hotel.

Entering the United States through passport control is an interesting experience. It seems that everyone is suspected of being a potential terrorist. The same could not be said of the French authorities. One could be the spitting image of Bin Laden at the height of his infamous activities and still be waved through nonchalantly by an unsuspecting border official. Not in America. In my case I was confronted with a large female uniformed official who lacked any sense of humour and was not particularly welcoming. Feeling a little nervous I decided to break the ice as she poured over the details of my passport.

'Good afternoon and may I say how nice it is to be here in America.' The warmth of my greeting was not reciprocated.

'You're not there yet. What is the purpose of your visit to the United States?'

'I am the leader of a school trip to visit Washington', I responded with the confidence of someone who was going to be allowed to proceed through border control imminently. I was wrong.

'Wait there for a moment sir.' At that point she removed herself from her seat to reveal a backside that was at least half the size of the state of Texas. She returned with another officer who was studying my passport as he walked towards me. He checked that my passport photo corresponded with the real thing. He was also holding another piece of paper, which had an official look about it.

'Mr Punknowle?'

'Yes, that is I?' The entire tour group had already made their way through passport control and were gathered together on the other side waiting for me to join them. They, including the Ferret and Slabb, appeared to be enjoying my discomfort. I was becoming irritated.

'Mr Punknowle, have you visited the United States before?' Anyone would think I was trying to enter North Korea.

'Yes, I think it was two or three years ago. Is this some sort of survey you are conducting officer?' There was no response.

'Can I ask why I am being treated in this fashion? I am a subject of her Britannic Majesty and yet you treat me as if I were some sort of common criminal.'

'You are.' I continued with my protestations until I realized what he had just said.

I was now becoming concerned that some of my activities back home had been detected, but I decided that attack was the best form of defence. An outraged approach was necessary.

'How dare you? I have never been subjected to this sort of treatment anywhere in the world, not even in France!'

'Sir, when you were last in the United States you failed to pay a parking ticket.'

I was given the option of an on the spot fine of a thousand dollars or to appear the following month in the courtroom in Madison County, Virginia. Immediate deportation was another option. A thousand dollars was removed from the tour fund and I was permitted to enter the United States.

The travel company had organised a coach from Dulles to the centre of Washington. On the coach we were joined by the travel company representative. Although he was well into his fifties he was wearing a baseball cap with the word *'Sox'* embroidered just above the peak. Going by the name of Elmer Krackerwitz he supported a large moustache that along with a hotdog waistline made him look rather like a walrus. This gentleman was to act as our guide whilst in Washington. Looking out of the coach window it would appear that skis and snow boots would be required when visiting the sights; there was snow and ice everywhere.

The journey to the hotel took rather longer than I expected and we didn't arrive until 4 o'clock. Our place of abode for the next four nights, *The Welcome Hotel*, was situated on 11th Street on the corner of M Street. One would have thought that a country that had landed men on the moon would be capable of coming up with more original names for the streets of its capital city. Richard Nixon Avenue springs to mind. The hotel had the advantage of being situated only five blocks to the north of the White House. I slipped slightly when I got off the coach; the city council had obviously failed to apply grit to the pavement. Upon entering the hotel lobby it was apparent the décor was somewhat threadbare and in need of a lick of paint. The Ferret looked particularly unimpressed.

Elmer the Walrus was lingering in the lobby. With a degree of sarcasm I asked if he was waiting for a tip.

'No, I'm just making sure the checking-in goes ok and then I thought we could discuss your itinerary for tomorrow', he replied with an air of self-importance.

'Mr Ferris is entirely capable of overseeing the rooming arrangements. As for the itinerary, I will issue you with your instructions tomorrow morning. Be here at half past nine sharp. Goodbye.'

Elmer the Walrus was momentarily stunned by my direct approach, but I deemed it important he knew who was in charge. From his expression I knew he had taken an immediate dislike to me.

'Ok Sebastian, I'll be here in the lobby at nine thirty on the dot.'

'Thank you, but would you kindly address me as Mr Punknowle.'

After a bit of a glare he turned and without saying another word made his way to the revolving doors.

I knew, from previous experience that sorting out the rooms would be very frustrating and therefore I had entrusted, or rather lumbered, the Ferret with the task. While the Ferret was still resolving the issues of which boys should go into what rooms, Slabb and I had gone up to our rooms to freshen up and partake of a bourbon on the rocks . After about half an hour there was frenzied knocking at my door. Attired in my relatively new quilted smoking jacket I opened the door to find a very irritated Ferret.

'Tim, what on earth is the matter?' I tried to appear genuinely concerned.

'You could have hung around to help me.'

'Problems?'

'You can say that again!' I was not wrong in assuming there would now be long list of complaints. Naively believing the issuing of the keys would represent the conclusion of the rooming assignment, the Ferret had received delegation after delegation of students complaining about their rooms. The main issue appeared to be their refusal to share double beds. There were three beds in each room. There was also only one shower in a room with no door or curtain arrangement. Also, the one lavatory in the bathroom lacked a seat. The double discomfort was not lost on me. Knowing the Ferret and Slabb would be enduring similar facilities brought on the Punknowle smirk.

Also, many of the boys had brought condoms on the trip. Even before unpacking Wayne, among others, had filled them with water and bombarded passing pedestrians in the street below their windows. The Ferret was thus subjected to a tirade of abuse and the occasional threat of legal action in full view of the other hotel guests in the lobby. He was also informed by the hotel manager that a repeat of any such behaviour would result in the group being asked to leave the hotel. I believed this to be the main objective of the boys.

After the Ferret had calmed down a little I proceeded to issue him with instructions.

'Tim, would you kindly inform the boys that they will either have to share a bed or sleep on the floor. You might suggest they sleep at opposite ends of the bed. You may think about doing that yourself with Augustine.'

Obviously the Ferret had forgotten about his own sleeping arrangements. The thought of what I had just suggested had made him close his eyes and cringe. I continued.

'With regard to the condom issue, would you ask Augustine to deal with it. He needs to stress that the condoms are not to be used for such activities. After all, they are not cheap.'

A little confused by the point I was making, he proceeded to ask what I was going to do.

'I thought I would unwind in a hot bath with a bourbon and soda and contemplate the agenda for tomorrow.'

'Is that all?' His reply struck me as a tad impertinent.

'Tim, my dear chap. You must understand the task of a group leader is not an easy one. It is imperative that I prepare myself for the rigors that lie ahead. You must also be ready for our busy day tomorrow; you do look very tired. After you have spoken to the boys I suggest you go for a short nap before we go out for dinner.'

It was about eleven o'clock at night in Britain and I was entirely aware that a short nap would develop into a deep sleep, which would probably end at three o'clock in the morning with the Ferret being wide awake. Not only would this result in jet lag for the poor Ferret, but also I would not have to be subjected to his company for the rest of the evening. However, he seemed more than happy to accept my advice.

I was to thoroughly enjoy the evening, especially as the Ferret had failed to show up at the meeting point in the lobby. It was left to Slabb and me to take the group to Union Station via the underground Metro system. Although the building still serves as a railway station, about a hundred shops and a food court have been added in recent years. It was in the food court I was joined by Slabb and Wayne to enjoy some delicious Maryland crab cakes, which were washed down by a couple of bottles of dry white wine from California. Wayne, however, had nearly caused a scene when he was informed by the waiter that he was too young to imbibe alcoholic beverages. The threat of teeth removal failed to persuade the waiter to amend his decision. Slabb advised Wayne to let the matter rest and have some *coca cola* instead. In order to make up for his disappointment at not having any wine Wayne followed up his crab cake with a rather large burger and fries.

It had been an eventful day and by eleven o'clock we were all ready to return to the hotel and a good night's kip.

12

The next we saw of the Ferret was nine o'clock the next morning over a bacon and egg bagel breakfast in a diner just round the corner from the hotel. The Ferret had awoken at about half past three and found it impossible to get back to sleep. Jet lag certainly played a part, but Slabb's constant snoring and gurgling noises didn't help. The Ferret looked awful and would have been very happy to return to the comfort of his bed *sans* Slabb.

Elmer the Walrus was in the lobby at the appointed time armed with a rolled up golfing umbrella. However, there was no sign of the rest of the group. I was aware Slabb was up in his room scrubbing his shirt clean after breakfast. The Ferret had also gone up to collect his camera. When both colleagues were back downstairs I instructed them to go back up and rouse the group from their slumber. I then turned to Elmer the Walrus.

'Mr Krackerwitz. Today I want us to have a tour of the White House, followed by a walk to the Washington Monument, followed by a stroll along the Reflecting Pool to the Lincoln Memorial. Also, if there is sufficient time I would like us to make our way to Arlington Cemetery. '

'I'm afraid that's not possible', he replied with a contemptible smugness.

'And why not, pray?' Clearly this could develop into a conflict of wills.

'We do not have the tickets for a White House tour.'

'Surely, not an insurmountable problem? From where do we procure them?'

'From the White House Visitor Center. It's just across the way from the White House.'

'Well, go and get some then. We'll need twenty eight. I'll wait here for the others.'

'Well Mr Punkkowle, it's not quite that simple. To stand a chance of getting any tickets you need to start queuing at three o'clock in the morning, and by now all the tickets would have gone. The earliest you can get on a White House tour will be at some stage tomorrow.'

Obviously I was not very impressed. 'Mr Krackerwitz, will you make sure you are at the Visitor Center at three o'clock tomorrow morning to get the necessary tickets.'

'I'm afraid, Mr Punknowle, that's not part of my job. I'm contracted to start work at eight o'clock in the morning.'

'Oh very well then. The Reverend Slabb and Mr Ferris will have to do it. Mr Ferris awakes at that time anyway. I suppose I can hold the fort here.'

Eventually the rest of the group appeared in the lobby, wanting to know the venue for breakfast. They were told they were too late for breakfast; we had to start our route march round the sights of Washington. Upon leaving the hotel I walked at the front with Elmer the Walrus; we were followed by twenty five hungry and grumbling teenagers and Slabb and the Ferret brought up the rear. Before very long there were stragglers in the column and there was something like two hundred metres between me and the rear of the group. It reminded one of Napoleon's retreat from Moscow in 1812. Inevitably, Wayne was the very last and was being shunted along by the Ferret. Turning right onto Pennsylvania Avenue it was not long before we reached the railings of the south side of the White House, just across the road from a large grassed area known as 'The Ellipse.'

Through the railings one could make out the six columns of the central part of the building. Either side there were shrubs and trees and between the White House and the railings there was an immaculate lawn with a fountain as a centre piece. It was an impressive sight. Had I been an American I would certainly have set my eyes on the presidency. There is no doubt I would have been a Republican. Unfortunately the present incumbent was a feeble liberal Democrat.

The Ferret, the tour official photographer, took a series of snaps through the railings. There was the customary group photograph in front of the White House. Some of the boys made some indecent gestures and Elmer the Walrus tried to be involved in the photograph until I ushered him out of the way. There were also a significant number of blue-uniformed policemen around. From the badges on their shirts it was possible to make out they were M.P.D.C. officers (Metropolitan Police, Washington DC). Elmer the Walrus also pointed out there were also Park Rangers on duty around the White House. I had supposed Park Rangers could only be found in the Yellowstone National Park to stop people from feeding the likes of Yogi Bear. I noticed how overweight these law enforcement officers seemed to be. I suppose, however, they were not in the habit of chasing likely offenders; they simply shot them from a distance.

We then made our way to the north side of the White House via 15th Street and the Treasury Building onto Pennsylvania Avenue. We were closer to the White House on this side and it was just possible to make out the West Wing where the Oval Office is located. The Ferret continued to click away with his camera. He took several shots of the façade and the famous colonnaded portico where the president greets other world leaders. Perhaps one day in the future I would be greeted as Prime Minister of Great Britain. I pointed out the White House roof to the Ferret and he was very happy to oblige and take pictures of the top of the building including the security systems and Secret Service officers.

On the other side of Pennsylvania Avenue was Lafayette Square. In the centre of the Square is a large statue of President Andrew Jackson. Elmer the Walrus was keen to explain the significance of Lafayette and Jackson in American history. I instructed him not to bother, especially as both men were responsible for British military defeats in former times. Lafayette was that French chap who was responsible for Britain losing America in the War of Independence. He had become friendly with George Washington and arranged for a whole load of French soldiers to come across the Atlantic to help the American rebels defeat Cornwallis at Yorktown in 1781. Andrew Jackson was responsible for defeating the British at the Battle of New Orleans in 1814. This little scuffle took place in the War of 1812-14, when the British marched on Washington DC and burned it to the ground. Apparently the Battle of New Orleans was fought after hostilities had ended and therefore as far as I am concerned it should not count on the military score sheet.

In each corner of the Square there is a statue of a foreigner who fought with the Americans in the War of Independence – two Frenchmen, one German and a Pole. Well at least the German has two good reasons to regret the creation of the United States! I informed the Ferret there was no point in taking pictures of this insignificant plot, but I was ignored. I was also ignored by Elmer the Walrus, who, while waving his umbrella around in dramatic fashion, was giving a group of my boys the American version of events. I marched over to the Walrus gathering.

'Time to move on Bilgebury; we have much to see today without taking in trivial sites of American history.'

'Hardly trivial, Mr Punknowle!' Clearly Elmer the Walrus was going to be a problem.

'Mr Krackerwitz, would you kindly do as I ask. I do not appreciate your gloating and my group has absolutely no intention of celebrating the demise of the British Empire in North America.' Wayne led the applause.

While crossing over Pennsylvania Avenue I was nearly knocked down by an old age pensioner on a skate board. With only one arm, he was using his only available hand to brush his teeth. From a distance it looked not dissimilar to a case of rabies. Safely across the road we made our way to the Ellipse past the Old Executive Building on 17th Street. It was rather too French looking for my liking. If I wanted to see French architecture I could have taken the group to Calais and saved an awful lot of dosh. I instructed the Ferret to take a picture of a rubbish bin on the pavement in front of the French inspired heap.

'What on earth for?' The Ferret was obviously bemused.

'I want our photographic record to reflect an entire American experience. We need to take pictures of a whole range of things – buildings, monuments, letter boxes, ordinary Americans going about their normal daily lives, taxis, and yes, rubbish bins.' Slabb nodded his approval, and even the Ferret and Elmer the Walrus were persuaded by the force of my argument. Oddly enough, so was I! From that point on the Ferret was happy to take photographs of almost everything he came across including post boxes, school buses, policemen, even someone eating a bagel!

Our next stop was the Washington Monument. One is able to see this pile of white stone from almost every part of the city. I allowed Elmer the Walrus to bore the group half to death while I was having a coffee break in a nearby café. He apparently rambled on about the various stages of construction. Slabb informed me afterwards that the US government had run out of cash in 1848, and it was twenty years before they could think about completing the project. No such problems with Nelson's Column!

The Reflecting Pool was something of a disappointment. There was no Reflecting Pool! All the water had been allowed to drain away. Perhaps the government had run out of funds again. The Lincoln Memorial proved to be a very impressive site. I would like such a construction to immortalize the record of my own achievements as Prime Minister. Parliament Square in Westminster would be a perfect spot. The statue of Winston Churchill could look up at me. However, I would want them to build it before I popped my clogs, otherwise what's the point.

By the time we finished at the Lincoln Memorial everyone was somewhat fatigued. It was at this point Elmer the Walrus broke the habit of a lifetime and became useful. He suggested we take the Metro Blue Line to Arlington Cemetery. Not unlike the London Underground, the Washington Metro system had its fair share of interesting station names. The boys were particularly amused by the station with the name of *Foggy Bottom*! Having visited the site of President Kennedy's grave and the Tomb of the Unknown Soldier, the group leader decreed it was time to return to the *Welcome Hotel* and prepare for our evening meal in a catering establishment known as the *Hard Rock Café*.

Over the next couple of days we were to visit a number of historic sites around the city including the Jefferson Memorial, the Supreme Court, the Old Post Office Building on Pennsylvania Avenue, the US Capitol and the Library of Congress; Wayne, as a matter of principle, remained outside. Everyone also enjoyed the visit to the National Air and Space Museum on the Mall. During lunch on the third day Wayne announced he was fed up with the history stuff and wanted to go shopping. Feeling the need for a break from the deliberations of Elmer the Walrus, I agreed that the group should have some free time in the afternoon. I also wanted to do a bit of shopping so I took myself off with Wayne to Pentagon City, a large shopping mall in the city suburbs. Slabb took the opportunity to visit the Washington National Cathedral and last resting place of President Woodrow Wilson. The Ferret was quite content to continue clicking his way round Washington to record the 'entire American experience.' Elmer the Walrus was dispatched home with instructions to meet us at the hotel the following morning at nine o'clock.

Pentagon City had a fascinating array of shops and it was clear to me that I would be able to achieve my objective without too much trouble. In the meantime I was dragged by Wayne into a men's fashion store by the name of *Mollisters*. We were met just inside the entrance by a young chap in his twenties who was not wearing a shirt. His greeting struck me as being somewhat unusual.

'What's up?' While asking this rather odd question he was slouching against the counter. This would never have occurred in a Marks & Spencer Menswear Department.

'Nothing is up actually, apart from the fact I can't see anything.' The entire shop was almost in darkness. Had sales been so bad they had been forced to cut down on utility costs? Had pay for its employees been cut? After all, the individual at the door was not the only one not wearing a shirt.

It soon became obvious that the sales assistants had been employed by the company for their looks and not for any knowledge of the retail industry. In a John Lewis menswear department a sales assistant would hound you around the rails and hangers in an effort to achieve a sale. This was not the case in this fancy establishment. You were simply ignored if you were older than twenty-five. Even if you fell within the age range there was no guarantee of getting any assistance. One employee was dumbfounded when some poor soul asked about the location of socks. Without the aid of a torch I managed to feel my way to the shirts and I picked out a suitable item and proceeded to try it on in a changing room. Finding the changing area proved more difficult than first supposed; I had been sent the wrong way by one of the male models who spent most of the time admiring themselves. It proved impossible to get the shirt on; it did not enjoy quite the same cut as a shirt from *Moss Bros*. On returning the shirt to one of the assistants I was somewhat rudely informed they did not have any XXXL in stock. Rather than continue stumbling around the dark cave I headed for the safety and light of the pedestrian area to await Wayne. His quest for clothing proved more successful than mine and he emerged from the dimness with four carrier bags.

At this point we went our separate ways. I needed to procure a number of items and I preferred to do so alone. By the time I met up with Wayne my purchases included a book on how to create homemade surveillance tools and weapons, a pair of binoculars, a tool kit, a black woollen balaclava, a pair of black leather gloves and a copy of the Koran.

The next morning we all met in the lobby at the appointed hour. This was the last day of the trip and we were due to fly home at ten o'clock in the evening. There were to be two excursions today, but we didn't have sufficient time to do both. I decided that Elmer the Walrus and Slabb would take half the group to Mount Vernon, the home of George Washington. The remainder of the group would go to another location with the Ferret and me.

'Where are you off to then', asked Slabb, afraid he was about to miss out on something exciting.

'A little place by the name of Brandywine Creek old boy.'

'Brandywine Creek. What's all that about then?'

Rather too many questions from the Chaplain for my liking, but I kept my composure. 'It's the site of a battle where the British defeated George Washington in the War of Independence in 1777.' Elmer the Walrus was not looking convinced. However, everyone else seemed content and so we set off in minibuses in different directions out of the District of Columbia.

On the way to the destination I couldn't help but notice that the Ferret looked worn out. I don't think it had anything to do with the daily itinerary, but more to do with the nocturnal activities of the Chaplain. In rather graphic terms the Ferret described how in bed Slabb would stroke his ankles with his sock-covered toes. This was too much information so soon after breakfast. When the Ferret moved onto tongues and dribble it was time to bring the conversation to an abrupt conclusion.

A few miles out of Washington heading south we began to see signs for *Andrews Air Base*, the home of the president's aircraft, *Air Force One.* As predicted the road passed directly past the air base. Once we could see the hangars and some military aircraft I instructed the driver of the minibus to park on the side of the road. For security reasons there was no lay-by or official viewing points.

'Go on Tim, take a few snaps of the base.' Once again the Ferret was happy to oblige.

'The entire American experience!'

'Absolutely old man, absolutely.'

Feeling pleased with his latest set of images we proceeded down the road to Brandywine.

Once we entered the town the minibus driver asked where exactly we wanted to go. Having informed him of the destination he drove around the town for about ten minutes failing to find any road signs or references to any battle at Brandywine Creek.

'Are you sure this is where we want to be, Sebastian?' The Ferret was becoming anxious.

'Well, this is Brandywine; the Creek must be somewhere around here.'

The Ferret politely asked the driver to come to a halt at the side of the street. He had decided to seek directions and picked on an elderly couple who had just emerged from a hardware shop. At first there were expressions of confusion and then there was suddenly a *eureka* moment on the part of the gentleman. The woman, whom I presumed to be his wife, started to nod in apparent agreement. The Ferret returned to the minibus.

'You have brought us to the wrong place.'

'Oh?' I appeared startled by this revelation.

'A battle was never fought here during the War of Independence or, for that matter, in any war.'

'But I'm sure there was a battle fought at Brandywine Creek.'

'There was.'

'There you are. I knew it.' The Ferret drew breath.

'It was fought miles away to the north near a place called Wilmington on the way to Philadelphia!'

There was silence on the way back to Washington. There was no time to go to the real Brandywine Creek and the Ferret was sulking as a result of missing the trip to Mount Vernon.

We returned to the *Welcome Hotel* by about lunchtime. The Ferret was eager to get his packing completed before Slabb returned from Mount Vernon. In the lobby there were a number of police officers and four other serious looking chaps in suits. Two of the men and a police officer approached the Ferret and I. He produced a silver badge in a leather holder. I noticed the hotel receptionist nodded in the direction of the Ferret.

'Mr Timothy Ferris?'

'Yes', came the reply from a very concerned Ferret.

'Sir, my name is Agent Edwards. I am with the FBI.' The Ferret greeted this information with stunned silence. The FBI agent continued.

'Sir, acting upon intelligence received today the FBI obtained authority to search your hotel room and your personal belongings. Having conducted our search we are satisfied you represent a threat to the security of the United States. As such we have no alternative but to take you into custody.'

'This is ridiculous', pleaded the Ferret. He was then asked to surrender his camera. The contents only confirmed their suspicions. At that point the Ferret was read his rights and handcuffed by one of the uniformed police officers. The Ferret was led away just as Slabb and Elmer the Walrus returned from Mount Vernon.

'What on earth has happened?'

I turned toward the Reverend Slabb. 'It would appear that the Ferret is a terrorist.'

13

By the time we arrived back at Lord Bilgebury College the Ferret's arrest was already headline news. He was the fourth item on the BBC's *Look East* news bulletin. He did even better on ITV's *About Anglia.* The *Cambridge Evening News* had produced a front page feature on the Ferret's alleged activities. However, the Anti-terrorist Squad had raided the Ferret's home and had found nothing to link him with any terrorist activity. As he lived off the College campus I had been denied the opportunity of planting any incriminating evidence prior to leaving for Washington. The suggestion had also been made by members of the boarding community that the Ferret could be linked to Read's murder. Although the Ferret would have been unable to explain the presence of those suspicious items in his room in the *Welcome Hotel* the evidence against him was pretty circumstantial, even flimsy. Images of litter bins, postal boxes and hangars at Andrews Air Force Base may have been of some interest to the Department of Homeland Security, but it was hardly enough to send the Ferret to Guantanamo Bay to await the fate of a military tribunal. That would be too much to hope for! Indeed it was assumed that he would soon be released and repatriated.

However, his problem would now be one of credibility in the Lord Bilgebury community, at least in the short term, and therefore an immediate return to the College seemed unlikely.

This hypothesis was confirmed by the Headmaster at an emergency staff meeting at the start of the new half term. Very probably the Ferret would return at some stage, possibly at the start of the new academic year in September. However, it was also certain that the Ferret would never be the headmaster of Lord Bilgebury College. A case of mission accomplished!

The past few months had been very difficult for the Headmaster. It had all started with the dispatching of Guy Straker, the neo nazi historian, to Inverness. Then of course there had been the murder of Donald Read. There was also the injury to Theodore Clapp, who had still not sufficiently recovered to resume his duties as Examinations Officer. And now he had the Ferret crisis to deal with. The staff and parent body were beginning to feel the College was jinxed. It was also clear the national and local press were about to weigh in with their views on the happenings at Lord Bilgebury College.

All of this was bad news for Grover-Smythe. An independent school depends on pupil numbers to survive. Lord Bilgebury College had nearly closed during the recession of the 1990s; pupil numbers had fallen to about 270 by 1997. However, as the economy improved so did the prospects for Lord Bilgebury College. As Grover-Smythe had been appointed Headmaster in 1998 he was able to claim the credit for the ever improving numbers on the College roll. By 2010 there were 450 pupils receiving some form of education at Lord Bilgebury College. However, once again the economy had fallen into recession – a deep one. Inevitably there was concern about pupil numbers. Indeed by the start of the present academic year the number of pupils had fallen to 428, with a further fall predicted for the start of the next academic year.

The College's public examination results were not helping the situation either. They had steadily improved in the first few years of Grover-Smythe's stewardship, but recently the College Governors, egged on by Mrs Noggins, were expressing their concern at falling pass rates at GCSE and A level. There was a genuine fear now that the recent spate of scandals would bring about a nose dive with regard to pupil numbers. Grover-Smythe had even informed the housemasters he had received a worrying number of letters from parents informing him they were thinking of withdrawing their sons from the College.

Obviously I wanted to replace Grover-Smythe as Headmaster, but I didn't want the College to collapse in the process. I was very much aware that I had been the cause of some of the College's recent problems and I decided it was now prudent to postpone any future activities in an effort to arrest the decline in Lord Bilgebury's fortunes. My plans for Fotheringay and Grover-Smythe would have to be put on hold until the future of the College was secure once more. It was in this spirit of magnanimity that I invited the Headmaster and other College notables around for dinner with the purpose of conducting a council of war. Grover-Smythe was very happy to accept.

Invited to this gathering of great minds was me, the Headmaster, David Fotheringay, Augustine Slabb and for some extraordinary reason, Russ Dicker, the Director of Sport. His inclusion was the Headmaster's idea. The agenda was to be put together by the Headmaster and therefore my task was the nosh. Muriel, my cleaner, agreed to prepare the meal. Two days before the feast I sat down with Muriel to discuss the menu. We ran into problems straight away with the starter.

'Muriel, I thought that after the canapés we could have gravadlax with dark rye bread.'

'You what?', came Muriel's reply in a broad fenland accent.

'Scandinavian pickled salmon.' I felt a translation was required.

'I don't know about that Mr Punknowle. For starters me and Sid always have prawn cocktail or oxtail soup for posh dinners.' I had never had the pleasure of meeting Mr Pluggit.

'It's very simple Muriel. Go and see Mr Sprigg, the fishmonger, and he will slice the salmon for you. I think we should have some mustard dill sauce to accompany the salmon.'

'Is that a sort of seafood sauce, Mr Punknowle? Sid loves that stuff. Quite often he mops it up with a slice of bread.' Clearly, this was not going to be straightforward. I handed her my *Delia Smith* cookbook and suggested she simply follow the instructions.

'What about the main course, Mr Punknowle? I do a very nice steak and kidney pudding. Sid can't get enough of it.'

'I'm sure he can't Muriel. No, I thought we would have Tournedos Roquefort served with asparagus.' Muriel again looked bemused.

'What about a bit of mash with it?'

'No, the asparagus will be just fine.'

'Mr Punknowle, would you mind if I asked my sister Peg to give me a hand with this. She's got an O level in French.' My suggestion of apple pie for pudding was greeted with a sigh of relief. With an air of confidence Muriel asked if the pie should be served with custard, ice cream or both. I suggested *crème anglais* would suffice. Once again Muriel was out of her depth.

The following morning I paid a visit to the Conservative Association office. I had arranged to have a meeting with the Association Agent, Rupert du Flapp. He is the chap employed by Conservative Central Office to organize things for the Party in the Cambridge constituency. His role is to find candidates to contest local and general elections, fight elections, organise the selection of, and then look after the parliamentary candidate. Thanks to the Trotskyite tendencies of the students at Cambridge University, the city of Cambridge has a female Labour MP. The agent is also responsible for raising funds for the Party coffers.

I was shown into the Agent's office by Prudence, his rather elderly assistant. She was probably old enough to have voted for Stanley Baldwin in the 1936 general election. Rupert was not in the office but I was invited to sit in the chair opposite what I assumed to be his desk. Whilst waiting for Rupert to appear I took the opportunity to investigate the contents of this nerve centre of political organization. In pride of place upon the wall was a signed framed photograph of Margaret Thatcher. A portrait of Winston Churchill enjoyed a similar level of prominence. Although the desk was tidy the same could not be said of other parts of the office. There were old election posters, some dating back to 1979. The Union flag draped on the wall looked particularly sad as if it had been attacked by moths over a period of many years. There were stacks of undelivered election leaflets surrounding brown cardboard boxes that probably contained more literature that had not made it to the letter boxes of Cambridge. It was interesting to note there was no photograph of the present leader of the Conservative Party. I did not have to wait long before I was joined by the Agent.

Rupert du Flappe was in his mid-fifties but his oily silver hair made him look older. He was not tall, in fact only about five feet six inches. His waistline suggested he did not belong to a gym or a ramblers club. However, he was clean shaven and looked very neat in his double breasted navy blazer, grey flannel trousers, white shirt and predominantly blue tie. Judging by the shine of his black shoes it was obvious they were cleaned almost on a daily basis. Having lived myself in Taunton I recognized a West Country accent.

'Sorry to keep you waiting, Sebastian. I hope you haven't been here too long. I had to pop out for a new ink cartridge for the printer.' I suspected Prudence didn't have the faintest idea what an ink cartridge was. After the customary pleasantries we embarked upon the purpose of my visit.

'Rupert, what are the chances of me winning in Crankton?' I was hoping it was a safe seat, but I was disappointed in this respect.

'Very much a two horse race, I'm afraid.' Rupert filled the bowl of his pipe with *St Bruno Rough Cut* tobacco. 'The Lib Dems hold the seat at the moment, but we came a very close second, with Labour a long way behind in third. If we can get our supporters out we should be able to get the seat back.'

'Who is the Lib Dem candidate?'

'Chap by the name of Colin Anderson. He won the seat at the last election and by all accounts he's been doing quite a decent job on the Council.'

'What help can I expect from the local Conservatives?' Rupert lit his pipe.

'They're a keen group of people although I have to say they're getting on a bit. The Chairman of our branch in Crankton is Aubrey Sutton. Aubrey's eighty-three and regarded as a bit of a moaner. Hardly a week goes by when he hasn't sent a letter to a cabinet minister complaining about one thing or another. He's not a great supporter of the present government. He's never forgiven them for getting rid of Maggie.'

To me the solution was easy, 'Why haven't you got rid of him?'

Rupert smiled, 'Not that easy. The other members of the group like him and I have to say he is a good organiser.' I knew I would have to visit Aubrey at some stage soon.

'Rupert, should I win the seat, might there be a chance of becoming the parliamentary candidate? I feel I have so much to offer the Party and the country.'

Rupert re-lit his pipe, 'It certainly wouldn't do your chances any harm. But nowadays we don't always get to select our own candidate. More often than not we have candidates imposed on us from Central Office.' I was not to be put off.

'How does one become a parliamentary candidate?'

'There are a whole series of hoops you have to jump through. You also have to be supported by two Members of Parliament. You send a letter of application to Central Office. They then ask you to attend an interview with the chap from

Regional Office in Norwich. If all goes well you get invited to a candidate selection board in London. The selection process lasts for three days.' Rupert didn't discourage me.

I left the Association office knowing that I would have to win in Crankton to stand a chance of becoming a parliamentary candidate. I would have to find a way of dealing with the threat posed by Colin Anderson and the Lib Dems before election day. I couldn't rely solely on the Crankton electorate to remove this barrier to my political ambitions. I also had the impression that Aubrey Sutton could hamper my chances of success at the polls.

Muriel and her sister Peg managed to produce something that looked and even tasted something like it was supposed to. David Fotheringay had played around with all the courses with his fork, but Russ Dicker appeared to enjoy the entire culinary experience. Everyone around the table would have noticed he was holding his knife as if it were a pen, thus betraying his working class origins. The Headmaster had supplied the wine, a very decent *Mageux*. Dicker consumed this fine Bordeaux wine as if it was half a pint of shandy. It was to be over a glass of brandy that we began our deliberations.

The Headmaster started by summarising the various crises that had befallen Lord Bilgebury since the start of the academic year. He also warned of the possibility of a visitation by the Independent Schools Inspectorate. There would be very little warning of such an inspection and Grover-Smythe stressed the importance of making sure that every aspect of the College was ready for the grey-suit-and-clip-board invasion.

The Headmaster looked around the table at his colleagues. 'Gentlemen, are there any suggestions as to how we can overcome this current crisis and restore the reputation of the College.' David Fotheringay was about to respond but he was beaten to it by the Chaplain.

'We can start by beating the MCC and Saffron Walden next term.' Grover-Smythe looked across to Russ Dicker.

'I'm sorry Augustine?' Grover-Smythe asked for clarification without really wanting it.

'In my humble opinion Headmaster I believe it would be foolhardy to get rid of cricket at Lord Bilgebury College. How can we be regarded as a place of serious academic endeavour and rigour when we don't play the game which is so much associated with the education of young Englishmen?' The Headmaster was stunned by the emotion displayed by the College Chaplain. He felt obliged to respond.

'Augustine, the youth of today do not want all of their Saturdays taken up by playing cricket. Russ knows how difficult it is to get out teams nowadays.' Everyone looked over to Dicker. He nodded his agreement with regard to the Headmaster's remarks. Slabb was not going allow this to drop.

'We all know that for some extraordinary reason you both detest the great game. This has nothing to do with raising teams. It is all to do with money. In an effort to introduce girls and to buy more javelins, relay batons and all the other bits and pieces you need to use on an athletics field, you are both prepared to deny our young men the opportunity to enhance their characters on the cricket field.'

'That's rubbish Augustine!' Grover-Smythe was becoming angry. 'We are here this evening in an effort to try and save this College. If we make our boys stay here to play bloody cricket every weekend they will want to leave!'

'Twaddle!' This was fighting talk from Slabb.

'And there's also our exam results to consider. The day after last year's MCC match we had the Geography Paper One GCSE exam. All those who played in that bloody match failed the exam!'

'I seem to remember Headmaster that most boys failed the second Geography paper last year, also; that paper did not follow any cricket match. However, am I right in saying that you taught Geography to Year 11 last year?' This was becoming messy.

'My decision is final. I have discussed it with the Board and cricket is going next year!' At this point the Chaplain got up and stormed out. One was reminded of the relationship between King Henry II and Thomas Becket. The King was to ask, 'Who will rid me of this turbulent priest?' Unfortunately the King was overheard by some of his loyal knights who took it upon themselves to slay the Archbishop of Canterbury!

Although Grover-Smythe did not advocate that we remaining three should go with haste to Primrose Cottage to put Augustine Slabb to the sword he was, nonetheless, very unhappy about the Chaplain's outburst. He continued to rant about Slabb until at last he regained his composure. He then re-turned his attention to the purpose of the gathering.

'Although Tim Ferris will hopefully be back with us at some stage in the future, his absence does mean we are a body short on the Senior Management Team.' Russ Dicker was looking hopeful. 'Sebastian, how do you feel about taking on Director of Studies at least until Tim gets back?' The promotion would be handy, but I was entirely aware that I was unsuited to the role – too much like hard work.

'Thank you, Headmaster, but I feel that the post of Director of Studies isn't really my forte. Someone like Peter Turner would be excellent. He would enjoy the challenge of doing the timetable for next year and there would be no need to make him Acting Director of Studies. After all, if justice prevails Tim Ferris will soon be released. Assuming, of course, he is found to be innocent of the serious charges against him.' Fotheringay and Dicker nodded their approval.

I think Grover-Smythe was impressed with both my modesty and my reasoning. 'The fact remains, however, that we are still short on the SMT.' Again Dicker looked hopeful. 'We need a strong team in these difficult times, especially as there may be an inspection just around the corner. I need men of calibre and principle around me.' Grover-Symthe nodded at David Fotheringay, who likewise responded with a nod of his own.

'Sebastian?'

'Yes Headmaster?'

'Both David and I agree we need you on the SMT. Would you be prepared to serve as Senior Master?'

14

I had entirely agreed with Slabb's sentiments but I deemed it sensible to keep my own counsel on the matter, at least for the time being. Since his verbal confrontation with Grover-Smythe, the Chaplain had kept a low profile and embarked upon a period of self-imposed exile in Primrose Cottage. When he wasn't sulking he continued to teach Religious Studies to his sixth form group and lead the services in the College Chapel. Beyond that it was naturally assumed he was being brow-beaten by Miranda Slabb more frequently than usual.

For my own part I was very happy to accept my promotion onto the Senior Management Team as the Senior Master. I now ranked number three in the College – quite an achievement in fewer than three terms. I was now earning a salary on a par with a junior executive in the City. My rather generous package took into account the fact I was still Head of History and the Housemaster of Hoare. However, I delegated much of the tedious administration in the History Department, such as text book and paperclip ordering, to Arnold Pryke. Aspects of the boarding house, such as the care and welfare of the boarders, didn't interest me and I was therefore happy to give the resident tutor more responsibility. As with the History Department, however, I still made the important decisions with regard to Hoare House.

I still had to teach and this was something of an inconvenience. Like most senior members of staff, in any school, I hated teaching and promotion was traditionally the method by which one escaped from the misery of having to instruct the adolescent members of the community. I was obliged to teach twelve, forty-minute lessons a week to the sixth form. This meant I only had twenty eight free periods during a typical week. It was almost akin to slavery.

My Year 13 History students had handed in their A level coursework assignments directly after half term. Owing to the idleness of the examination board, teachers are expected to mark the coursework scripts. The marking is merely checked by an examination board moderator to ensure accuracy and consistency; past experience would suggest that many don't even bother. Unlike the mug who actually marks it, the moderator gets paid by the examination board. Coursework represents twenty per cent of the overall assessment for A level. Almost without exception, the standard of work submitted by my students was dreadful. In times past I would have been content to give the lazy rotters the low marks they deserved. However, I was not unconscious of the fact their performance was a reflection upon my teaching. They therefore had to achieve decent marks in their coursework but I had absolutely no intention of helping the blighters. Well, I would not assist them personally. This has nothing to do with professionalism – I simply find the reading of their version of history an utter bore.

Fortunately, I had a chum who was a History research assistant at Pembroke College. I had known Courtney Brewer since our prep school days. After leaving Durham University with a First in History he had embarked on a number of career paths without success. His first attempt at employment was as a trainee manager with Tesco. However, he was relieved of his duties after refreezing the fish fingers. He very nearly wiped out half the population of Harrogate. Other jobs ended in varying degrees of failure. It was then decided he should go into academia where being a human disaster area didn't seem to matter.

Courtney was always short of cash. He had something of a gambling problem caused mainly by frequent visits to local betting establishments and horse racing at Newmarket racecourse. Also, at great expense, he was known to engage the services of ladies and, on some occasions, gentlemen of the night. I knew there was a way of both furnishing Courtney with much needed funds and sorting out a problem of my own. I therefore arranged a clandestine rendezvous with Courtney at St John's College on the Bridge of Sighs, which traversed the River Cam.

As expected, he was delighted to accept my proposition. Courtney would arrange for some History undergraduates to write the coursework assignments for my students at Lord Bilgebury. As far as the undergraduates were concerned it was to be an academic competition with the best effort, judged by Courtney, to receive a prize of one hundred pounds. In this way any undergraduate suspicions would not be aroused. I would pay Courtney a further five hundred pounds for his efforts. It was then my intention to obtain a reimbursement from the Lord Bilgebury History Department budget.

I was beginning to feel very content with life; everything seemed to be going to plan and I was looking forward to a future of academic and political power. Then, just a week before the end of the Spring Term, I was to be faced with a terrible dilemma. Albert Noggins had failed in an attempt to steal cigarettes for Wayne Flack from the local newsagent. As a punishment for this failure Wayne had tied Noggins to a chair, removed his shoes and socks and proceeded to sting him on the feet with stinging nettles. On this occasion, however, Noggins did not suffer in silence and reported the incident to his mother.

The very next morning Nancy Noggins, the crocodile, arrived at the College demanding to see the Headmaster. Grover-Smythe, through Lucy Dockett, informed the crocodile he was busy. In fact he was hiding in the toilet. As Fotheringay was away on a course, I was detailed to fend off the menacing reptile. She was invited into my office.

'Good morning Mrs Noggins. How may I help you?'

'You can start by getting rid of that boy Flack.'

She was obviously in no mood for pleasantries. I then sought to quell her fire.

'Have no fear Mrs Noggins. We are aware of the incident and the Headmaster has decided to place Flack in internal suspension for a whole day.'

In fact Grover-Smythe knew nothing of the matter. I knew Wayne would hate this punishment but what else could I do, faced with this formidable female?

'That's not enough. I demand the thug be expelled!'

This was turning ugly.

'Do you not feel, Mrs Noggins, that would be a little extreme? After all, we have no actual proof that ….'

'Proof? Are you calling my son a liar, Mr Punknowle?'

I had to handle this response with care.

'No, certainly not, but when talking about expulsion we must consider the legal implications.'

'Well Mr Punknowle, let me give you a legal implication of my own. If you do not get rid of this boy I will sue the College for not dealing with the obvious bullying of my son over a period of many weeks.'

I was wrong. I also knew that such a law suit would be the last thing that Grover-Smythe would want at the present time. He already had enough to contend with but I had to do my best to save Wayne as there could be serious implications for me.

'Mrs Noggins, I am sure you are a generous and forgiving person. I will, personally, make sure that Flack never touches Albert ever again. Furthermore, the College will suspend Flack for a week and then gate him for the rest of his time at Lord Bilgebury. We will also place him on a last warning.'

I thought this would do it. Wrong again.

'No, no, no!'

I suddenly realised that Nancy Noggins was the spitting image of the '*Spitting Image*' Maggie Thatcher.

'Mr Punknowle, as you know my husband is on the Board of Governors at this College and he has already brought the matter to the attention of the Chairman of the Board. Both my husband and Sir Fletcher Snogworthy are adamant that Flack should go without delay.'

I was certain the Headmaster would sacrifice Wayne to appease Nancy Noggins, especially as she had the support of the Board. The support of the Board of Governors was also something I would need in order to progress to the Headship of Lord Bilgebury. Wayne would have to go and I would have to find a way of making sure I didn't experience any fall-out from this unfortunate situation. The Headmaster did agree that Wayne should be expelled and I was tasked with informing Wayne and his grandparents.

Within a couple of hours of my phone call Wayne's grandfather arrived at the College. It was the first time I had met him. Well into his sixties, Mr Flack had something of an unkempt look about him, almost dishevelled. His hair displayed no evidence of any grooming and he had not shaved for at least two or three days. He had an engaging smile but this only revealed tooth loss and decay. His shirt collar was frayed and the state of his jumper suggested it was more of an old friend than an item of clothing. His brown trousers had not seen a crease for a considerable length of time. I had already made Mr Flack aware of the fate of his only grandchild. He had not been surprised. In fact, he was more surprised Wayne had lasted at the College for so long. I assured him that Wayne could still take his exams at the College in the Summer Term. I was thanked by Mr Flack for all I had done for Wayne and he apologised for his grandson having let me down. I was almost emotional. Mr Flack said he would inform Wayne of the College's decision but I persuaded him that I would like to speak to Wayne myself. Again, Mr Flack praised me for my caring nature. I was more concerned that Wayne didn't spill all the beans!

For the last time I showed Wayne into my sitting room. We both sat on the sofa that faced my plasma television set. I was reminded of all the times we had watched all those 18-rated movies together. Such pleasant memories.

'Wayne, I have some very bad news.'

'You 'aven't run out of beer 'ave you?'

I was relieved Wayne took the news of his departure from Lord Bilgebury very well. He could have made things very difficult for me. Indeed, during our chat on the sofa he intimated that he knew rather too much for comfort. In return I promised that he would do very well in his exams. He wasn't convinced this would be the case owing to a lack of determined study throughout the year. I said I had a plan in mind and once I had sorted things out I would inform him of my idea.

When the ordeal was over, Wayne returned to his room to pack. He also wanted to say farewell to Albert Noggins. About half an hour later I went to the Hoare House car park to bid farewell to the Flack family. Before Wayne got into the back seat of his grandfather's Daimler I quietly assured him that one day soon we would get even with Nancy Noggins. As the Flack Daimler made its way to the main gate I waved with a tear in my eye. But I knew I would meet Wayne again.

In sorting things out over Wayne's exams I had to make contact with Courtney Brewer once more. This time we met for a coffee in the Pembroke College Refectory. The coffee was to be extracted from one of those noisy machines offering a multitude of different forms of coffee. I pressed a button that indicated I was about to get a *cappuccino*. The first sip from the polystyrene cup made me think of a rugby sock in boiling water infused with low fat milk. I pushed the offending item to the middle of the table.

'Courtney, old man, I need another favour and it's not as straightforward as the coursework business.'

'Sounds intriguing. What is it you need?'

I was hoping Courtney was in need of more cash.

'Do you know any bright sparks who know anything about history, geography and business studies? It would also help if they are a tad corruptible.'

'I see.'

I had the feeling Courtney was already contemplating earning a substantial fee. I proceeded to inform him of my plan.

By the time I left the Pembroke College Refectory, Courtney had indicated that he could make the necessary arrangements. He also indicated it would not be cheap. I was to arrange for Wayne to sit his summer exams in other schools around Cambridge as a private candidate. Courtney's students would then sit the exams for Wayne. Not knowing what Wayne looked like, the exam officials in these schools would be none the wiser; as far as they would be concerned, the person sitting the exams would be Wayne Flack.

A few days later Courtney called me to confirm he had found three students who were prepared to stand in for Wayne. However, they were demanding payment of five hundred pounds each. For his administrative services Courtney had suggested a figure of a thousand pounds. Obviously ladies and gentlemen of the night were becoming more expensive or, perhaps, more frequent. I didn't have that sort of money in my bank account so I was obliged to withdraw the cash from my credit card. Should all my career plans come to fruition I was confident I could replenish the Punknowle coffers.

The Spring Term was now at an end. All my pupil reports had been written the week before. Well, one report had been drafted on my word processor and then copied and pasted thirty four times. The Flack affair had cast a dark shadow over what had been a reasonably successful term. At least Wayne would do well in his exams and I was confident he would remain silent with regard to our activities. It was now time to consider my political ambitions.

15

It was the first Saturday morning of the Easter holiday and I awoke at my normal time of twelve minutes past six. The Punknowle ablutions could be a little later this morning and therefore I decided to remain in a state of slumber. Unable to get back to sleep I started to think about the forthcoming election campaign and how I might counter the threat posed by my Liberal and Labour opponents. I dare not leave the outcome of the poll entirely to the ignorant electorate of Crankton. My deliberations were to be rudely disturbed by the sounds of an electrical appliance being used to suck up the dust and crumbs on the drawing room carpet. I had forgotten it was Muriel's cleaning day. It was pointless trying to think under such conditions so I made the decision to leave the comfort of my luxury bespoke double mattress. Although I was attired in my cream silk pyjamas I deemed it necessary to also wear my Noel Coward dressing gown.

Muriel was still vacuuming when I descended the stairs and ventured into my drawing room. I tapped her on the shoulder. 'Oh Mr Punknowle, you did give me a fright.'

'Good morning Muriel. You are very early this morning.' There was a hint of irritation in my voice.

'Yes, sorry Mr Punknowle, but I've got a lot on today and I wanted to make an early start.'

'I see, and what is so important to disturb me at this time of the morning?' I checked my pocket watch; it was just after seven o'clock.

'I've got loads of baking to do for next Saturday.'

'Saturday. What's happening next Saturday?' I wasn't very interested but it was something to do while I was trying to find my television remote control. When cleaning, Muriel had the annoying habit of changing the position of most items in the house, especially ornaments and remote control devices.

'It's the Crankton Spring Fete, Mr Punknowle. Me and Sid always run the cake stand; done it for years. All the money goes to local charities. It's quite a big thing.' I was becoming a little more interested.

'So there are quite a few people who go to the fete then?'

'Oh yes, Mr Punknowle. Most of the village will be there. That's why it's so important to get cracking with the cake baking. I can then put them in the freezer.'

'I might pop along myself.'

'You must do, Mr Punknowle. And you can buy one of my cakes too. You'll have to buy a jar of Beryl Arnold's home made plum jam. It really is gorgeous. And Sid loves going to look around Mr Anderson's second-hand book stall. He enjoys his crime novels.'

'Mr Anderson?' I was certainly becoming interested.

'Yes, that nice Mr Anderson always does the book stall. He's actually the District Councillor and does so much for the village.' This was even more of a reason to go to the fete.

'By the way Mr Punknowle, you need some more polish and bleach.' Muriel's return to domestic issues annoyed me a little as it disturbed my thought processes.

'Well, go and buy some.' 'Alright Mr Punknowle, but I'll need some money to get them from the little shop across the road.' I gave her the Punknowle stare.

'Take it from the money I pay you.' After all, I did pay her the minimum wage.

The following Monday I met up with Rupert du Flapp and Bertram Prior-Ashby, the Chairman of the Cambridge Conservative Association to discuss election strategy. Upon my arrival at the Association office I was introduced to Aubrey Sutton, the Crankton Conservative branch chairman, and his daughter, Melissa. Mrs Sutton was not present; Aubrey very swiftly informed me his wife wasn't at all interested in politics and was looking for a new washing machine in *John Lewis*. I deem it unnecessary to describe the physical features of Aubrey Sutton as most men in their eighties are of similar appearance.

I have to say I was immediately taken by Melissa who was about my age. Aubrey must have been over fifty when he fathered her. She was an attractive and perfectly formed woman with olive skin and auburn hair. She had lovely hazel eyes and dazzling white teeth. Indeed she seemed perfect in every way. Her dress sense was immaculate, as was the way she spoke. Not too tall, not too short she represented everything that Punknowle admired in women. True, these were only first impressions, but I was smitten. I asked myself could this woman be the potential Punknowle consort.

Before I had arrived at the office I had intended to inform Aubrey his services would not be required on the basis that his age would be a handicap on the campaign trail. Afterall, I saw myself as the trailblazer of progressive and dynamic conservatism. With Melissa now on the Punknowle radar it was impossible to dump the old chap. In order to impress Melissa, I was prepared to make her father feel that he was vitally important to my electoral prospects. This display of insincere respect encouraged the old chap to give us the benefit of his views. He launched into a tirade against the present Conservative government and its economic policies. He warned me that the idiot in 10 Downing Street could be responsible for me losing in Crankton.

'It's bloody stupid. That's what it is.'

'What is dad?' Melissa smiled at her father. We all awaited his response, if not with baited breath.

'These austerity measures, that's what. They tried all that in Germany in the 1930s, and looked what happened there – Adolf bloody Hitler! If they bloody cut public spending then jobs will have to go. If people get thrown out of work, they get unemployment benefit. And if they don't have a job, they can't get paid. If they don't get paid, they can't pay tax. Also, they can't buy anything. How's that going to stimulate the bloody economy and balance the budget?'

Rupert du Flapp gestured to respond but it was all in vain.

'And that's another thing. I sent a letter to the Chancellor of the Exchequer last week and I still haven't had a reply. Bloody man!'

Rupert made the mistake of asking what was in the letter. 'I asked him to give me a detailed analysis on whether or not Britain should come out of Europe. I rather suspect we would save a lot of bloody money. Let Johnny Foreigner get on with it I say. Let them have their bloody euros and measure their bananas and carrots. Let's get back to trading with the Empire.

It's an absolute bloody disgrace the way we dumped them to join that bloody lot in Europe. During the war we fought alongside the Aussies and Canadians against the bloody Germans and Italians. And you can't deny New Zealand lamb is better

than that scrawny French stuff. I mean it's not even lamb is it? Lord knows what you're getting. That beef we had for lunch last Sunday – well, it didn't taste like beef to me. Probably donkey from Spain, or some other third world country.'

It was decided that we should start canvassing the following week. Rupert had suggested that by then all the election literature would be printed and ready for delivering. I asked Melissa if she would canvass with me on a couple of afternoons. She replied that she would be delighted to. Unlike her mother, she enjoyed the cut and thrust of politics.

During the week I busied myself with election planning. I went to the council offices to collect an electoral register for the Crankton ward. There were about eighteen hundred people registered to vote of which, according to Rupert du Flapp, only about forty percent would be bothered to turn up to the polling station at the local primary school. It wouldn't be possible to visit every household in the ward and nor did I want to. Crankton included a number of council dwellings, which had not taken the opportunity of becoming private homes as a result of legislation passed in the Thatcher era. The people living in these and other social housing were bound to vote for that woman socialist candidate. I would restrict my canvassing to nice middle and upper class homes where there was less danger of catching something nasty.

Rupert had also given me some useful intelligence on wheely bins, the scourge of twenty first century British life. Residents in Crankton, along with those in other villages, were unhappy about the collection of their rubbish. It was collected by the Council every two weeks, and it was felt this represented something of a health hazard. I was also aware that owing to Aubrey's cuts in public spending the Council could not afford a weekly collection. Giving the matter a good deal of thought I came up with what I deemed to be a vote winner. Homes that were worth more than two hundred and fifty thousand pounds could have their refuse collected on a weekly basis. Poorer people, who lived in cheaper housing or on the council estate, would have their bins emptied every three weeks. I reasoned that wealthier people had more purchasing power and therefore more waste.

I also spent a considerable amount of time thinking about Melissa. I had never known 'love' before, and I was never quite sure as to what it was. I don't think my parents had bothered very much with it. Father would turn the television off if any one as much as embraced on the screen. Mother informed me once that when she and father went to the cinema to see *The Sound of Music*, father walked out in disgust when Captain von Trapp kissed Maria in the garden summer house. He nearly refused to pay his television licence one year after watching a programme where two men were found in bed with one another. Father was eventually persuaded to pay the licence by mother who explained it was an American programme. I was certainly smitten by Melissa and perhaps I was experiencing the notion of love at first sight. Certainly, the prospect of matrimony would not do my future ambitions any harm, especially when one considered the quality and charm of the prospective Punknowle consort.

I next came across Melissa at the Crankton Spring Fete on the Saturday afternoon. She was with her parents. I was introduced to her mother, who, like her daughter, had dark hair and an olive complexion. Rupert du Flapp had explained to me a few days earlier that Mrs Sutton was Maltese. Aubrey had met her on the island in the 1960s while he was serving in the Royal Navy. After a very short courtship Aubrey had proposed and they were married in a small church in a village just outside of Valletta. I estimated that Mrs Sutton was about twenty years Aubrey's junior.

It was a very warm spring day with hardly a cloud in the sky. The grass was green with a freshness of smell, which suggested it had been cut by the village grass cutter that morning. As Muriel had described the week before, there was a wide selection of stalls and stands, offering the local community the opportunity of buying all sorts of items, ranging from Muriel's cakes and buns to gardening equipment. Aubrey and his wife went off to have a look at Mrs Arnold's jams and preserves, and I was permitted to escort Melissa around the fete.

While we were wandering around the fete, Melissa informed me she was a solicitor. Contrary to my first impressions, she didn't live with her parents, but owned an apartment in Crankton. She was very close to her parents and that is why she had chosen to study Law at the University and then work in Cambridge after graduating. My attraction to her only became stronger. I was about to invite her for tea in the refreshment tent when the tranquillity of the afternoon was disturbed by a loud bellowing in my general direction.

'Mr Punknowle, Mr Punknowle!' It was Muriel. I wanted to just politely wave and move on, but Muriel was having none of it. We were beckoned over to the cake stand.

'Good afternoon, Muriel. This is Miss Sutton, a friend of mine.'

'Nice to meet you, I'm sure.' Muriel winked at me. I responded with a disapproving Punknowle stare.

Before I knew it, Muriel and Melissa were engrossed in conversation about coffee and walnut cake and other such matters. As their dialogue progressed to Victoria sponge I noticed that Mr Pluggit was still busy serving the local populace. Certainly, Muriel's cakes seemed very popular. Fivers and pound coins were going into the shoe box with a considerable level of frequency.

'You appear to be having a busy afternoon, Mr Pluggit?'

'Oh yes, Mr Punknowle. We always do. They all love Muriel's cakes.'

'I can see that. I hope you're taking care of all that money.' I pointed at the shoe box.

'Oh no problem there, Mr Punknowle. Every so often either me or Muriel take the cash over to the organiser's tent to be looked after by Horace Smedley.'

Having been persuaded to procure one of Muriel's Dundee cakes, Melissa and I continued to make our way around the fete. Melissa did a splendid job by introducing me to a number of potential voters, although I was a little surprised that many were unaware of the election. It was not long before I came face to face with my Liberal Democrat opposition,

Colin Anderson. Although in his fifties, Anderson was still handsome. Muriel had likened him to Robert Redford, and I must admit I could see the resemblance. Trim, about six feet tall, he had a full head of blond but greying hair. He had a healthy tan and I had a problem. The female vote alone would be sufficient to scupper the Punknowle prospects at the polls. I presented my credentials, only to be greeted like a long lost friend. This was very disarming and even I was starting to like the fellow. However, I soon restored to myself a sense of mission, and informed Anderson I looked forward to the forthcoming contest. He merely continued to smile and chat away to adoring female pensioners.

At five o'clock the tannoy system announced the fete was about to be officially closed by Horace Smedley, the fete organiser for the past thirty years. At this point I informed Melissa I was in need of a comfort break. She continued to listen to Horace Smedley thanking everyone for their efforts. When I returned Horace was still droning on, but proceedings at last came to an end when Muriel was awarded the prize for taking in the most money for the day. Horace also announced the proceeds would be handed over to various children's charities in the south Cambridgeshire area.

I was in the process of saying my farewells to the Suttons when there was something of a commotion. Horace Smedley came running out of his tent in a state that could not be described as composed. Without attempting to calm himself he explained what had happened. 'It's gone, all of it! The tin with all the day's takings has gone! The money's been stolen!' When Horace had gone to officially close the fete he had carelessly left the money box unattended in his tent.

The next morning, following a tip-off from an anonymous source, the Police had discovered the empty money box in the wheely bin belonging to Colin Anderson, the Liberal Democrat candidate. He was arrested on suspicion of theft, but later in the day released on bail, pending further Police enquires. He claimed he knew nothing about the taking of the money box or the whereabouts of the missing cash. I agreed to make up for the theft by making a large personal donation of two thousand, five hundred and twenty seven pounds. In doing so I won the admiration of Melissa and hopefully the gratitude of the voters of Crankton.

16

The last two weeks of the Easter holiday were largely taken up by electioneering. Rupert du Flapp had suggested I canvass in the evening, but I wasn't having any of that nonsense. After dark I was far too busy ripping down LibDem posters. Also, during the day I found it much easier and quicker to canvass on the basis that most people were out at work. Again I reasoned that if the lady of the house had to go out to work, the chances they were Liberal or Labour voters was pretty high. Although Melissa advised to the contrary, I restricted my canvassing to properties that had at least four bedrooms. Houses with three bedrooms were, I believed, the hotbed of middle class liberalism. For the same reason bungalows were given a wide birth.

On a few afternoons some of the elderly ladies of Crankton would invite me in for a cream tea. I would be there for over an hour discussing my policies and the escalating price of budgie food. Rupert du Flapp came up with the ridiculous notion that these old dears were deliberately inviting me in for tea and a chat in order to stop me from canvassing. Apparently it was a typical Liberal trick at election times. I was having none of it; most of the time *Earl Grey* or *Darjeeling* was served in the finest china and with no hint of half fat milk. The strawberry jam for the scones was also homemade and therefore it was obvious they were Tory supporters. Not many of these ladies had a car so I offered to give them a lift to the polling station on Election Day.

On certain afternoons it was impossible to do any canvassing because I was invited to attend garden parties hosted by the great and the good of Crankton. Melissa and I spent a particularly pleasant afternoon with Lord and Lady Firbank, who had arranged a garden party in the grounds of their sixteenth century Tudor manor house in my honour. The garden was like a smaller version of a country park with its grand and immaculate lawns. In the distance there was a small lake, and it was just possible to make out four swans on the water. Behind a large hedge Lord Firbank assured me there was a swimming pool and a tennis court. He and Lady Firbank no longer played the game but during the summer holiday the honourable grandchildren would play the odd set or plunge themselves into the pool. Five well-to-do members of the Crankton set came along to meet their Conservative candidate. They all assured me of their support, but unfortunately four of them were unable to vote because they would be staying at a villa in Villefranche-sur-Mer in the south of France at the time of the election. This was something of a disappointment but still preferable to knocking on the door of complete strangers, even if they did live in four bedroom houses.

Again, upon the urgings of Melissa, I spent a considerable time at an establishment caring for the elderly. No politics was discussed and I was obliged to talk about the unpredictable nature of the British weather and the goings on in *Coronation Street* and *Emmerdale.* After a mammoth two hour experience of tedium, I eventually asked the old ladies and gentlemen of the Rose Hall Care Home if they would vote for me. Without exception they indicated they would. The visit had not been a waste of time after all. As I made my way out I popped in to the main office to inform the matron that I would arrange transport for the residents on the day of the election. However, much to my annoyance I was informed by the matron that the Labour candidate had already been to visit and had taken away their postal votes for processing. When I enquired as to why I was not informed about this when I first arrived, the matron, who was obviously a socialist agent, informed me that I had not asked. She also assumed I had visited the care home out of the kindness of my heart and not for any selfish political gain. When elected I would review public spending on this particular facility.

Of course I did the odd bit of canvassing and knocking on the doors of considerable properties and, for the most part, I received a positive response. There were some precarious moments on the door step, however. For example, when soliciting the vote of Brigadier and Mrs Ponsonby, their golden Labrador, named 'Monty,' took a particular liking to my left leg. Whist discussing the problems associated with the Crankton High Street potholes, I was obliged to contend with a canine humping experience. When the ordeal was over, and my dignity restored, I promised to look into the pothole outrage.

As the election drew closer I was confident of a resounding victory over my opponents. The LibDems had kept a low profile since the theft of the fete charity money, and in any event the electorate of Crankton were not likely to support a candidate who was still under police investigation. Labour had never done well in the ward and were expected to perform poorly again in this election. The election was set for the first Thursday after the start of the Lord Bilgebury Summer Term. To comply with the Representation of the People's Act I was allowed to be absent from the College on the day of the election.

The day for the village of Crankton to decide arrived, a day that would surely represent the start of a glittering political career. I had written my victory speech the night before as I knew I would be busy on the historic day. I had consulted my *Great Speeches* book to draw inspiration from the likes of Winston Churchill, Ronald Reagan and Richard Nixon. The speech, I felt, should not be a long one; I had in mind about half an hour. Modesty would not allow a prolonged oration.

Uncle Rex and cousin Perkin had driven up from Taunton the evening before. Uncle Rex wanted to do his bit for the Punknowle cause and thus he put his racing car green 1936 *Morgan* convertible at the disposal of my campaign. Cousin Perkin was persuaded to remain at my house as the classic car was only a two seat model. Also, I felt the rather tight fitting yellow *Star Fleet Captain Kirk* uniform he was wearing would only encourage the Liberal Democrats to come out and vote. As we drove out of the College gates at eight o'clock in the morning on our way to campaign headquarters, Uncle Rex's CD system was proudly and loudly playing *Land of Hope and Glory*. When we reached Crankton, Uncle Rex stopped playing his medley of patriotic music and produced instead a loudhailer. With one hand on the steering wheel, his other hand brought the loudhailer to a close proximity with his mouth, 'People of Crankton. Vote Punknowle! Vote

Conservative!' This would be repeated several times throughout the day.

Campaign headquarters was the Sutton residence. Upon being admitted to the Aubrey abode I immediately went over to embrace Melissa. 'Aubrey, Melissa, meet my Uncle Rex.'

Uncle Rex strode forward to shake Aubrey's hand with a firm grasp, 'A pleasure, sir.'

'Very nice to meet you, Mr Punknowle. This is my daughter, Melissa.'

'Oh, Rex, please,' Aubrey nodded his acceptance of the change of status, 'Charmed ma'am, charmed.'

Over coffee we discussed the programme for the day. Aubrey was just about to launch into a brutal attack upon the government's defence review, when Melissa came to our rescue. Aubrey continued to slurp his coffee and look for the biscuit he had just eaten.

'Rex, I was so sorry to hear about your school. Sebastian told me all about it. Was very much destroyed in the fire?'

'Yes, I'm afraid so. About a third of the School went up in flames. Tragic, very tragic.'

I too wanted to appear sympathetic, 'Yes, especially as that part of the School had only recently been refurbished with brand new desks and chairs, not to mention the vast bank of new computers.'

Melissa gently held Rex's hand, 'Never mind, I'm sure things will soon sort themselves out.'

'Of course they will my dear. The insurance will take care of everything.' Uncle Rex, appreciating her genuine concern, smiled at Melissa. However, for some unknown reason he appeared a little puzzled.

'OK everyone, to battle!' Everyone responded to the Punknowle call to arms and set about their election day tasks. Melissa's job was to co-ordinate those who recorded the people who came to vote at the polling station. Our canvassing in the previous few weeks suggested we could expect the support of at least five hundred voters, easily enough to win the election. Melissa's job therefore was to compare the voting intention of these people with the actual number of declared supporters who turned out to vote.

Aubrey's main task was to man the phone and ensure our supporters voted. At times throughout the day, this didn't go to plan. On too many occasions, Aubrey became very abusive to the person on the other end of the line. He had a row with one branch member of the Crankton Conservatives and suggested they were not allowed to vote for me because they had yet to pay the annual membership subscription.

After a day of steady voting, Melissa phoned me from the polling station just after five o'clock. She suggested that based upon the canvassing data, I was on course to achieve a landslide victory. At this point I punched the air and Aubrey made for the fridge to remove a bottle of sparkling Italian wine. Even Mrs Sutton, who had been hitherto making sandwiches all day, joined in the early celebration.

'Well done, my boy,' Uncle Rex was clearly very happy for his nephew, 'Your dear father and mother would have been very proud of you. I hope nothing will spoil it for you.' This attachment to his congratulatory words was a little odd, I thought.

'Thank you, Uncle Rex. Hopefully this represents the start of something big.'

Taking the opportunity of one of Aubrey's frequent visits to the bathroom, Uncle Rex enquired about Melissa. 'Tell me Sebastian, is there something going on between you and that very charming young lady?'

'I cannot deny it, Uncle Rex. I do honestly believe that she may be the one.' Uncle Rex beamed his approval.

In between Aubrey's berating of ministers of the Crown, Uncle Rex and I continued to talk about my future plans with regard to politics and Lord Bilgebury College. Just before seven o'clock my mobile rang. It was Melissa from the polling station.

'Sebastian, I think we have a problem. There has been a surge in the voting.'

'Don't worry old thing. That's what people do in elections.' I couldn't see what the fuss was all about.

'Sebastian, you don't understand. These voters are returning from work, and we have never seen them before. They weren't canvassed. We don't know what their voting intentions are.' I still didn't appreciate there was a potential crisis.

'Fear not, Melissa, we'll be fine. After all, they're not going to vote for that crook Anderson, are they?'

'Perhaps not, Sebastian, but the people voting at the moment probably live in three bedroom houses and bungalows.' The Punknowle penny finally dropped. Heavy voting continued during the evening until the polls closed at ten o'clock.

At half past eleven I was joined by Melissa, Aubrey and Uncle Rex at the Crankton Village Hall for the count. The other candidates were also there with their supporters. I was a little surprised that Colin Anderson wasn't in handcuffs. Just after midnight the count had concluded and the Returning Officer indicated he wanted to announce the results. The pile of ballot papers on the table suggested a close result. There was great tension. The Returning Officer rose from his seat.

' I, Reginald Spratt, the Returning Officer for the Crankton Ward, do hereby declare the results in the election for the Cambridge District Council.

Anderson, Colin Martin, Liberal Democrat Party, 146 votes.

Jarvis, Sharon Jane, Labour Party, 373 votes.

Punknowle, Sebastian Horatio Norbert, Conservative Party, 381 votes.

I therefore declare that Sebastian Horatio Norbert Punknowle has been duly elected to serve as the District Councillor for the Crankton Ward.'

There was cheering from the small group of Punknowle supporters. Melissa gave me a hug. I kissed her on the lips. Uncle Rex was close to tears, and Aubrey was just about to start a row with the Labour candidate. Melissa pulled her father away from the potential fray. I shook the hands of my opponents and then moved forward to make my victory speech.

'Mr Returning Officer, I would just like...' That is as far as I got before the door of the Village Hall opened to reveal a man with a small metal box. 'Sorry for the delay, Mr Spratt. There was a serious accident in Trumpington Street and I had to do something of a detour. I'm afraid I got a bit lost in the process. Anyway, here are the postal votes.'

All eighteen postal votes were for the Labour candidate, Sharon Jarvis. They were sufficient to give her victory. It was all the fault of the Rose Hall Care Home, and those who dwelled in three bedroom houses and bungalows. I was the only Conservative candidate to lose that night and therefore my political aspirations were at an end. There was only Lord Bilgebury to consider now, and Melissa. She did her very best to comfort me in my hour of need, and at this emotional moment in my life, I felt the need for her tenderness and companionship. Uncle Rex drove Aubrey home in the 1936 *Morgan.* Both felt the need for a stiff drink. Melissa and I were happy to walk home to her father's house. We discussed the reasons why I had lost the election. It was clear that I should have listened more to Melissa's advice. Then we turned our attention to the future. This was the moment. It was starting to rain, but it didn't matter. Keeping hold of Melissa's hand I went down on one knee, 'Melissa, I know we have only known each other for a short while, but for my own part I know I am in love with you. I knew it on the first day we met. Will you do me the honour of becoming my wife?'

To my surprise she said, 'yes.'

17

In the election I had underestimated the challenge from the Labour candidate. I had successfully dealt with the threat from Colin Anderson, but I had not anticipated that LibDem supporters would simply transfer their allegiance to Sharon Jarvis. I suppose I could have ventured into less prosperous areas and run the risk of being mugged or contracting some foul ailment. However, at the end of the day would I really want to represent people who reacted to my generous donation following the fete theft with such ingratitude? I think not.

The election defeat was quickly forgotten as I began to look forward to tying the knot with Melissa. In keeping with the Sutton tradition of short engagements, Melissa and I agreed to set the date of our union for the first Saturday of the summer half term break. We would then proceed to our honeymoon destination. Although we agreed that we should get married in a registry office, there were disagreements over other aspects of the matrimonial arrangements. To celebrate our engagement Melissa and I went out for dinner in Cambridge. I knew of a lovely little restaurant on St. Andrews Street. Before we started the main course, there was a minor dispute over the honeymoon destination.

'I think you'll enjoy Monte Carlo,' I naturally assumed my choice of location would go unchallenged. I was wrong.

'Well perhaps we can think about the honeymoon at a later stage.' I was used to getting my own way.

'Don't you want to go to Monte Carlo then? We really need to discuss this now as I have to get on with booking flights, hotels and so on.'

'I just think Monte Carlo is very pretentious. I would just like us to begin our married life in a less ostentatious setting.' I never considered Monte Carlo to be pretentious or ostentatious. I just like being around wealthy and attractive people.

'Where would you like to go then? Benidorm?'

'Don't be silly, Seb, of course not. I was thinking more in terms of the Alps; like Switzerland or Austria.' This was the first time she had used the shortened form of my name. Was she perhaps getting above herself?

'The Alps? I'm not too sure about that.'

'Why ever not?'

'I don't want to spend my entire holiday trudging through snow and ice. In any event I don't ski.' Melissa started to laugh. 'And what is so amusing, pray?'

'They don't have snow in the summer, silly.' This was the second reference to the word 'silly' and I didn't like it.

'I would still prefer to go to the south of France, but if you are so determined to go yodelling in the mountains then so be it. The soon to be Mrs Punknowle can have her way.'

'That's another thing, Seb.'

'What is?'

'I want to keep my maiden name of Sutton.' I very nearly brought up my smoked haddock mousse starter.

'What's wrong with Punknowle?'

'Absolutely nothing is wrong with it. I just want to keep my own name.'

'What will people think? Uncle Rex will be horrified.' I wasn't best pleased either.

'I don't really care what other people think. It's what we think that's important. And Uncle Rex will just have to get used to it.'

'He might, but I'm not sure I'll be able to.' Melissa realised I was upset about the issue and attempted to take the heat out of the situation.

'Don't worry, Seb. Our children will have the Punknowle name.' I was in need of a large gulp from my glass of *Chablis*.

'Did you say children?' This was the first time I linked the subject of children with regard to my proposed union with Melissa.

'Yes, I think I would like one of each,' was her matter of fact response. I had another gulp of wine before making my response.

'Well, perhaps we can think of having children a bit later on, say in four or five years or so.' I realised there could be no blocking this idea. The best I could hope for was to postpone the start of the family Punknowle. Unlike other people who longed for a family, I could not see the joy of having children in my life. Let us consider the life cycle of an offspring. Firstly, there are the sleepless nights. The baby stage of existence is notoriously noisy and smelly. There then comes the expense of prep school and Saturday mornings of watching football and cricket being played badly. The teenage experience is one of more expenditure, truculence and loud 'music'. This period is expensive owing to the necessity of a boarding school. The prospect of having a teenager around in the evenings would be too much to bear. The truculence and defiance would be experienced during the long holidays. Then there is the cost of sending them to university. It is hard to believe it was a Labour government that introduced tuition fees. When they eventually complete the Surf Boarding degree and reach adulthood they proceed to think their parents need to be treated like children. They seem to think the world began the year they were born. Life without children seemed more preferable.

'Seb, I'm nearly thirty seven. I can't afford to wait too long.' I didn't really enjoy my rare to medium fillet steak with peppercorn sauce.

On the Monday following the election, Grover-Smythe called an emergency Senior Management Team meeting. When Lucy Dockett showed me into the Headmaster's study, David Fotheringay was already there. The meeting meant I had to leave my Year 11 class, which was something of a relief as they were expecting some assistance with revision for their forthcoming History GCSE exam. I had forgotten what I had taught them over the course of the year. I knew it was something to do with Stalin, but I couldn't be sure. I left them to watch a *Star Wars* DVD.

Grover-Smythe informed us that the Independent School's Inspectorate (ISI) had contacted the College to inform us they would be inspecting Lord Bilgebury the following week over a period of three days. This was an inspection that Grover-Smythe knew the College had to pass. There wasn't long to prepare for the inspection, and David Fotheringay was given the task of preparing the academic side of the inspection, whereas my remit was to be pastoral. Over the next few days, therefore, I would be reviewing areas such as boarding, food and the spiritual life of the College.

The ISI team arrived the following Monday carrying their black brief cases, laptop holders and tablets. A computer mouse was dangling precariously from the trouser pocket of one of the inspectors. In the good old days there was plenty of time to prepare for a school inspection as there was at least six month's notice. This gave schools sufficient opportunity to paper over the cracks. Unmarked exercise books and essays were marked, CRB checks were carried out on members of the teaching and ancillary staff. Also, department meetings were held in classrooms rather than down the local pub, teachers started to register their classes for attendance and disciplinary matters were recorded on the computer system and so on. Before the notice of an inspection very few of these things were attended to, especially in a mediocre independent school such as Lord Bilgebury College. In the modern era schools had to contend with on the spot inspections, thus limiting the time and opportunity to cheat. But I would do my best.

At four o'clock, Fotheringay and I had tea with the Headmaster to assess how the first day may have gone. By all accounts David Fotheringay had had a harrowing experience in the first few hours. I tried to ease his pain.

'It couldn't have been that bad, David?' Grover-Smythe looked on anxiously awaiting his response.

'You wouldn't believe it. For a start, take Period Two Physics. The Inspector was told to expect a lesson on astronomy. Instead the class were shown a *Star Wars* DVD for the whole forty minute lesson!'

'Oh dear,' came my insincere reaction. Grover-Smythe held his head in his hands.

'That's not all. In History Period Four, one of the Year 12 students asked Arnold Pryke why the Poles had revolted against Russian rule in the nineteenth century. After some hesitation Arnold responded the Poles didn't like Russian winters!'

'Dear old Arnold.' The Headmaster didn't respond well to my attempt to diffuse the situation. 'Dear old Arnold be damned. He needs to be pensioned off, and bloody quickly.'

Fotheringay continued with his tales of woe. 'During the morning break one of the inspectors asked about drama productions at the College. He was informed by our Head of Performing Arts that rehearsals would start on *Robinson Crusoe* the following week. When asked about the nature of the somewhat limited cast, Patricia Pooke said that the Headmaster had been critical of the amount of money spent on the *Oliver* production the previous year, and wanted something less lavish this year.' I had never really liked Miss Pooke, but she was beginning to grow on me. Grover-Smythe merely stared at his tea going cold in the cup. Concerned over the Headmaster's health, Fotheringay decided not to mention the Potts fiasco at this stage.

During the afternoon there had also been problems in the Food Technology Department. Brenda Potts had been the Food Technology teacher at Lord Bilgebury for about two years. She had previously worked in the kitchens of a local *Little Chef.* Although having no formal qualifications apart from O levels in English and Maths, she had been appointed to Lord Bilgebury owing to the fact she was the only one to respond to an advertisement in the *Cambridge Evening News*. There had been some concerns raised about her academic results – no pupil had yet achieved a pass grade at GCSE. However, Food Technology was way down Grover-Smythe's list of priorities, and nobody had bothered to investigate the reasons for this lack of success. After observing her lesson, the Inspector reported back to Fotheringay. I overheard the feedback.

'There appears to be a problem with Mrs Potts.'

'There is?' Fotheringay pretended to be unaware of any serious issues.'

'I am afraid that Mrs Potts seems to know very little about food or its purpose.'

'Really?'

'She seems to think that food isn't a significant aspect of the course. She tends to place too much emphasis on the technology.'

'Well, that's not so bad then?' Fotheringay was starting to feel the situation could be rescued. This was perhaps premature.

'I wouldn't say that necessarily. She seems to believe that technology refers to the electrical appliances used in cooking. The entire lesson was devoted to turning on a microwave oven. According to her scheme of work, next lesson the pupils will learn how to operate a toaster.'

'So nothing about food, then?' Fotheringay had resigned himself to the fact Brenda Potts would not be scoring an 'excellent' for her teaching skills.

'Well, she did warm up some soup in the microwave, which she consumed while the pupils were doing their Geography homework.'

Things had obviously not gone well for David Fotheringay on the first day of the inspection. He had done his best to ensure there weren't any disasters on the teaching front. Like any school, Lord Bilgebury College had its fair share of poor teachers, and for the duration of the inspection Fotheringay had arranged for certain teachers who fell into the 'unsatisfactory' category to be absent from the College. Some were hastily sent on courses; others were instructed to pretend they were ill and stay at home. Fotheringay also tried to get rid of the most disruptive pupils whilst the inspection was in progress. Again, this was another opportunity to remove inadequate teachers as they were required to accompany the naughty boys of the College. Unfortunately this particular ploy backfired. One bunch of our rowdy louts was let loose at a county championship cricket match between Essex and Middlesex at Chelmsford. One of the younger, less experienced, teachers had allowed a group of Year 10 pupils to wander off round the cricket ground by themselves. After about an hour the teacher was awoken by the public announcement system requesting him to go to the Members section of the pavilion to deal with his drunk and abusive charges. While he was rescuing the Essex Members from their Lord Bilgebury ordeal, other pupils charged onto the pitch completely naked to disrupt the progress of the Middlesex second innings. Needless to say the streaking episode was to feature on the ITV evening bulletin, *About Anglia.* The third item on the news programme, it was inevitably seen by the Inspectors in their lodgings at *The Royal Cambridge Hotel.*

For the second day of the inspection, the scrutiny would fall on me and I hoped I would fare better than my more senior colleague. Unlike Fotheringay, I had devoted all my energies into preparing for my aspect of the inspection. With regard to boarding I had made sure all the rooms in Hoare House were up to scratch. I demanded that all the floors were cleared of clothing. The boys never bothered to put their clothes away in the wardrobe or their chest of drawers as it was much easier to use the horizontal form of closeting. It was the first time many boys had seen their carpet for over a week. Much of the bedding had not been changed for several weeks. Pillow cases were stained with gel or by dirty and greasy hair. Once white sheets were now an off-creamy shade, covered with biscuit crumbs and cigarette burns. The cleaner removed a half eaten sausage from one bed. Posters of nude females were taken away to be replaced by maps of the world and posters promoting inspirational messages. Various detergents and scrubbing tools were used to wash away penises that had been etched on the walls. Empty beer and lager cans were removed from the window sills and any unfinished bottles of vodka found their way into the Punknowle drinks cabinet. In certain rooms knickers and brassieres had to be retrieved from underneath the bed. Clearly some of the boarders felt that entertaining the young cleaners was all part of the service.

In the Hoare House kitchen, the fridge was thoroughly cleaned for the first time in three years. A piece of festering cheese, also about three years old, was removed. Several hours were spent by the cleaners chipping away at remnants of burned pizza left in the oven. The usual sight of mouldy white bread was replaced by various forms of healthier products from the bakery section of Tesco.

Boarders had been bribed with their own House Funds to tell the Inspectors that boarding was a wonderful experience. They were also induced to express a high degree of satisfaction with their caring housemaster.

I was able to engineer a tour of Hoare House with the lead Inspector and he expressed satisfaction with what he had seen. He was also obviously impressed with my response to his questions. He was particularly pleased with my policy on bullying in the boarding house.

'I am totally against any form of bullying. In fact I adopt a policy of zero tolerance as far as bullying is concerned,' the Inspector nodded his approval, 'we had a situation only a few weeks ago when a Year 13 boarder by the name of Wayne Flack bullied one of the younger boys. I was appalled and went directly to see the Headmaster to demand that Flack be expelled. In confidence I have to say that our Headmaster is a bit weak when it comes to bullying and was quite happy to sweep the matter under the carpet.'

'What was your response to that, Mr Punknowle?'

'Being a man with high principles I made it pretty clear to the Headmaster that I could not accept his decision. I was left with no option but to threaten to resign if the bully was not expelled. Mr Grover-Smythe was obviously aware of my resolve and Flack was asked to leave the College. I received a lovely letter from Mrs Noggins, the mother of the boy who had been bullied, thanking me for the stand I had taken.'

'A brave stand, Mr Punknowle, but absolutely the right one.'

'Yes, I thought so. But I would be very grateful if you didn't make reference to our conversation with the Headmaster. He is quite a spiteful individual and I wouldn't want to lose my job over this. If I was without work I couldn't continue with my donations to several children's charities.'

'Don't worry, Mr Punknowle, I will be very discreet'.

On the last day of the Inspection the focus was on the spiritual welfare of the pupils. At my suggestion, however, Augustine Slabb turned his interview with the Inspectors into an opportunity to criticise the Headmaster over his decision to end cricket at Lord Bilgebury the following year. Slabb, still seething over his locking of horns with the Headmaster at my brain storming dinner party, suggested Grover-Smythe was not a true educationalist and lacked moral fibre. He further pointed out the Headmaster was only interested in profit making. The Inspectors were astonished to learn that Grover-Smythe had banned Holy Communion at the College. However, Slabb failed to point out this was a on -off situation due to the Chapel having vital repair work completed on the roof.

The pupils and staff were surprised and pleased with the improved level of catering during the inspection. Angelica Smite had treated the Inspection as if it were a visit by the Red Cross to a prisoner of war camp in Germany during World War Two. When the inspection was over the College returned to the usual dreary concoctions produced in the underground world of the Smite Empire.

I managed to come through the Inspection process unscathed. Even my observed lesson went reasonably well. Let's face it, anyone with a half a brain can turn on the style for only forty minutes. In this sense any ISI or Ofsted inspection lacks a certain vigour. Lord Bilgebury College managed not to fail the Inspection. In addition to the disasters, the Inspectors had witnessed some good things too. However, the inspection report did criticise the leadership of the College. The report was at pains to point out that this did not mean the middle management of the College. Grover-Smythe was to be on the receiving end of some pretty harsh comments made by the Inspectorate. It was the sort of damning report that leads to early retirement or a move to a quieter and smaller school in somewhere like Lincolnshire. The day after the Inspection team left, Grover-Smythe called to see me in my office. As I poured him a glass of dry sherry he thanked me for my efforts before and during the Inspection. He confided that he had a fight on his hands once the Board of Governors had read the full report. He also pointed out that the inspection report would have been much worse had it not been for my professionalism and loyalty.

18

I had been expecting that Uncle Rex would be my supporter at the registry office. However, when I had spoken to him over the phone about arrangements he informed me that, regretfully, he was unable to attend owing to business commitments. I was surprised and saddened by this news. I wasn't aware that Uncle Rex had any business interests apart from the farm and usually his farm manager, Walter Trull, dealt with the commercial aspects of the production and distribution of milk.

I have, for some extraordinary reason, very few friends, and therefore finding a replacement for Uncle Rex proved something of a problem. I had considered Augustine Slabb, but I knew Miranda would not allow him to be associated with a civil ceremony. In any event England were going to be playing New Zealand in the Second Test at Lord's on that particular Saturday and at the time of the ceremony Slabb would no doubt be in the locality of St John's Wood. Peter Turner would have hummed his way through the entire proceedings, and Russ Dicker would probably have lost the ring as easily as his brain cell. Eventually I decided that Courtney Brewer should have the honour.

The registry office passed off without any major mishaps. Melissa wore a very acceptable frock, although I wasn't sure about her hat. It seemed to resemble a poorly constructed bird's nest. From within the nest sprouted a number of black feathers, which looked as if a crow had crashed on landing. There were few witnesses; Melissa's parents were in attendance as was Courtney who was very nearly too late for the start of proceedings. He explained that a male 'guest' had been rather reluctant to leave in the morning. After the formalities had been concluded we took the short walk to the *University Arms Hotel,* just off Parkers Piece, a large grassed area in the centre of Cambridge. In the lavish setting of the hotel restaurant we celebrated the marriage with a couple of bottles of *Charles Heidsieck* champagne and a cold light luncheon. After a few words from Aubrey, Mr Punknowle and Ms Sutton made their way by taxi to Stanstead Airport to catch their honeymoon flight to Austria and the mountains of the Tyrol. Thus began a week of misery.

Although the flight to Salzburg was incident free, the transfer from the airport to the resort of Mayrhofen was a gruelling experience. After a three hour coach journey through the Alps we were eventually dumped off in an Alpine village by the name of Jenbach. From there we had to endure an hour in a taxi, arriving at our hotel, the *Elisabeth,* just before midnight. The hotel was probably named after the Empress Elisabeth, the consort of Emperor Franz Josef of Austria. There was no opportunity for a meal, so some form of Austrian sausage and gherkin sandwich had to suffice. This was washed down by a glass of local plonk going by the name of *Welschreisling.* I was reminded of the time, several years ago, when some psychopath in Austria decided to add antifreeze to wine. I wondered upon drinking this stuff, apparently from the

Danube plain, whether or not the same nutcase had been recently released from prison, and was back to his old tricks.

After surviving the antifreeze scare, Melissa and I proceeded to make our way to our room. Within seconds of entering the room I pointed the remote control in the direction of the television. Melissa was not amused.

'Seb, what on earth are you doing?'

'I am trying to find the cricket score on the *BBC World News.*'

'What the hell are you doing that for?' I would have thought the answer to that question was obvious. Even so, I couldn't quite work out why she seemed so annoyed about it. I assumed she was tired after our very busy day and wanted to get some sleep.

'Last night England finished up on 256-3, and therefore I wanted to see what progress has been made today. I could try phoning Slabby if you prefer?'

'This is the first night of our honeymoon, and the only thing you can think about is cricket!'

The penny had dropped and this was the moment I had been dreading ever since Melissa brought up the subject of children. During our short engagement we had never discussed sex. Melissa had probably assumed I was doing the honourable thing and waiting until we were married. The truth of the matter was that I had never experienced sexual intercourse. The prospect of engaging in such an act disgusted me. Also, I had absolutely no idea as to what to do. Father was always too embarrassed to discuss the subject and restricted any dialogue on the matter to an incomprehensible mumble about the birds and the bees, and left it at that. I received no formal, or even informal, sex education at school, and I gave up Biology at the end of the fourth form because I had fainted during the dissection of a dead rat. I had never been interested in girls ever since Maisy Reynolds pulled my trousers down in the middle of a corn field when I was thirteen years old.

Now I was in the middle of Austria with Melissa expecting me to do the deed without so much as an instruction manual. I had ventured into *Waterstones* book shop before we came away but there was nothing to be found. As Melissa was in the bathroom preparing herself for a night of passion, I was just hoping that she would initiate the distasteful process and that things would happen without too much of a contribution from me. According to the movies it didn't appear to be a difficult operation and if Uncle Rex could do it then anyone could, even me. I lay in bed nervously awaiting Melissa to emerge from the bathroom.

The next morning we went down to breakfast together. We didn't exchange any words from the moment we got out of bed to sitting down at the breakfast table. The previous night had been a disaster and it didn't get any better for the rest of the week as far as nocturnal activities were concerned. I broke the silence by describing the breakfast scene. There was a selection of bread although the most popular choice among the guests was the white round rolls. There were numerous jams and preserves although I was disappointed there was no sign of any orange marmalade. Many guests piled the various meats onto their breakfast plates. I later discovered some guests, mainly the British ones, were taking the ham and sliced sausage to fill their rolls for a packed lunch. However, a notice on the restaurant wall made it clear that this practice was strictly forbidden. Cooked food was also available in the form of scrambled egg, burnt pieces of bacon and very odd looking sausages. There were also items of food to appease the healthy types such as fruit and low calorie cereal.

We ate our breakfast mainly in silence and once again it was left to me to start up a conversation.

'So what's on the agenda today, then?' Melissa gave some thought to my question while she was digesting a grapefruit segment.

'I thought we could go for a walk along the river to Zell am Ziller,' I felt she wanted to add if you are man enough for it, 'We can then get the steam train back to Mayrhofen. The guide book says it's about eight kilometres to Zell with a decent footpath by the river.'

The last thing I wanted to do was go for a long walk. I was still tired as a result of the exertions of the day before. I didn't sleep very well either; our duvet was no larger than a pillow and I was disturbed in the early hours by the sound of cow bells. The cable car station was located to the rear of the hotel and people were being transported up the mountain as early as seven o'clock. The noise of this *Where Eagles Dare* operation also had a negative impact on the Punknowle attempts to sleep. But to keep the peace and get myself out of the 'dog house' I agreed it was a good idea. The truth of the matter, however, was that it was a lousy idea. It poured with rain all the way to Zell am Ziller and by the time we arrived there I had blisters on both heels. Melissa had made me buy some walking boots before we came away. I failed to take her advice and wear them in before we left. Worse was to come. Melissa, who enjoyed the outdoor experience, insisted we should walk back to the hotel and not bother with the train.

'Must we?'

'Well, if you feel you can't cope, then take the train. I'll meet you back at the hotel.' My manhood was being challenged again.

'Alright, if you insist, we can walk back.' Melissa was already on her way before I had finished my sentence.

About halfway back along the river I was really struggling. My legs were tired, my blisters were very sore and I had the start of a stomach upset. Melissa was the picture of health and vitality. It was not long before the situation became desperate. I was in urgent need of a lavatory, but there was no such facility in sight. Fortunately, before very long, we came upon a small railway station where we waited for the next steam train to Mayrhofen. My stomach problem was not easing and by the time the train pulled into the station I was close to an embarrassing accident. Leaving Melissa on board, I jumped off the train and made my way to the station toilets with considerable haste. The door to the toilet required a fifty cent coin to open it – I didn't possess one. I dashed to the station shop where I bought a postcard of a mountain. The cost of the postcard was fifty cents and therefore by handing over a one euro coin I was expecting to receive a fifty cent coin in change. The lady in the shop handed me a ten cent coin and two twenty cent coins. I begged for a fifty cent piece – she didn't have one in her till.

After a difficult walk back to the hotel, it was not long before I was able to clean myself up. It was decided to throw my boxer shorts and a new pair of rambling trousers in the

Mayrhofen municipal disposal facility. Once again I had proven to be a disappointment to my new wife.

Before supper I took the opportunity to try and get the test match score. Melissa was in the bathroom. The BBC World News proved to be useless; it was more interested in the Cuban economy than developments at Lord's. Even the sports bulletin restricted its reporting to American baseball and wild boar hunting in Germany's Black Forest. The weather forecast concentrated on the sub-continent of Asia – not much use for central Europe!

Supper in the hotel was very acceptable and was made up of five courses. The waiter managed to find a reasonably decent bottle of Italian red wine, which was preferable to the disinfectant I was subjected to the previous evening. I was aware that the Austrians were on the German side during the Second World War. I noticed that in the dining room the waiters had something of a military bearing to the extent they wore their leather money wallets as if they were luger holsters. When I was struggling back to the hotel earlier in the day I came across the funeral of a local dignitary. There was a definite military theme to the occasion – uniforms, brass band, various flags and even a rifle salute. Clearly these German types had not lost their militaristic tendencies.

The rest of the 'holiday' was a mixture of rain, mountains and melancholy. It was becoming clear that Melissa regarded me as a disappointment. In addition to certain problems encountered during the night it was becoming very apparent that we had very little in common, and this led to more than a few heated exchanges. A mutual interest in politics was not enough to preserve a marriage. By the time we got to the end of the week we were very largely doing our own thing. On the Friday before we were to fly back home I took an excursion to Berchtesgaden, Adolf Hitler's mountain retreat. Melissa went instead to Innsbruck to view the sights of the 1976 Winter Olympics.

Berchtesgaden is actually in Germany just across the border from Austria. I had a walk through the town and could not help but notice the proliferation of bars and cafés. The large beer glasses and steins, not to mention the substantial slices of layered cake, topped with mountains of whipped cream would explain the average waistline of about forty two inches in Bavaria. And that was just the women!

The climax of the excursion was the visit to Hitler's 'Eagle's Nest', which is situated on the top of the Kehlstein Mountain. Here, Hitler would relax and, on occasions, entertain foreign leaders such as Neville Chamberlain. To reach the building, which is now a restaurant, one has to take a bus trip up the mountain by means of a single track road. From the bus park it is necessary to walk through a 124 metre stone-lined tunnel to a brass-lined elevator that takes visitors on another 124 metres up through the mountain and into the building itself. The Nazi Party had presented the 'Eagle's Nest' to Hitler on the occasion of his fiftieth birthday. From the viewing platform I looked across at the mountain scenery that Hitler would have viewed eighty years previously. I think Hitler had women problems and by all accounts, like me, he preferred to avoid the so-called pleasures of the flesh. If it was good enough for Hitler, then it was good enough for me.

Saturday morning arrived and thankfully it was time to return to England. Melissa and I were civil to one another but we had very little to say on the journey home. During dinner the previous evening we admitted we had made a big mistake in getting married without really knowing one another. We decided that when we got back to Cambridge we would go our separate ways. For the sake of appearances, Melissa agreed not to seek a divorce until I had become Headmaster of Lord Bilgebury College. I assured Melissa this would certainly be achieved by the start of the new academic year in September.

However, before that could happen I would have to decide upon a method of relieving Lord Bilgebury of its Deputy Headmaster, David Fotheringay. He was no fool and every care would have to be taken in arranging his demise. Once he was out of the way I could turn my attention to Walter Grover-Smythe.

19

I saw no more of Melissa, which was just as well as it was obvious to me I was not interested in anyone else apart from myself. There were some awkward questions when I returned to work but they were less painful to deal with than the prospect of having to share my life with someone else, and who was obviously a sex maniac.

With Melissa out of the way my objective for the second half of term was the removal of David Fotheringay as Deputy Headmaster. I had come up with a few ideas of how to remove him from the scene. One possible method would be to find a way of setting up Fotheringay with one of Courtney Brewer's female or male prostitutes. Fotheringay would never survive the publication of the photographs. However, this strategy could be quite expensive. A cheaper way of setting up Fotheringay would be to purchase a reasonable amount of cannabis resin and place it in his desk drawer. As Senior Master I could arrange for the Police to come in with their sniffer dogs. Only last term this method was employed to expel a boy in the lower sixth. I suppose something more drastic could be attempted such as tampering with the brakes of his VW Golf.

Dealing with Fotheringay was put on hold for a time as A level and GCSE exams were in full swing. I have never understood the British timing of external assessment. Why are important external examinations taken in the summer months? When teenagers should be taking advantage of the warm and long summer evenings in June, they are condemned to staying indoors to revise. The growing problem associated with hay fever only adds to the misery of the summer exam season. The most important drawback of having examinations in the summer, however, is that many young men are unable to play or watch cricket. I failed my Geography O level because I preferred to watch a one day match between England and Australia rather than engage in revision for glaciers and volcanoes. The same applies to January external examinations. How can Christmas and New Year celebrations and a period of universal overindulgence be considered appropriate preparation for the sitting of exams? I sent a letter to the Department of Education in January suggesting that March would be a more appropriate time to sit examinations. I received no reply.

The History A2 examination went reasonably well. I had photocopied four of five pages from a *Letts* revision book and fortunately my candidates were at least able to answer some of the questions set in the examination. However, Courtney Brewer phoned me in a bit of a flap just after lunch on the day of the History exam. I was informed that the wrong undergraduate turned up for Wayne Flack's History exam. An idiotic Economics student showed up to sit the exam. Courtney had given out incorrect instructions. Instead of giving the exam his best shot, the Wayne Flack imposter left the exam hall in Lensfield College without writing a word on the answer paper. Wayne would now certainly fail the History exam even if he performed well in the coursework element.

Needless to say, Wayne was far from impressed with Courtney's debacle when I phoned him the following morning. He said he needed time to consider his options and that he would get back to me with his thoughts on the matter. However, he warned me that, whatever he decided, it wouldn't be cheap!

My position as Senior Master gave me access to all the staff files and they enabled me to compile my own secret dossiers on my colleagues. They made interesting reading. Four years ago Peter Turner had been suspended for throwing a battery at a pupil in his Physics lesson. On another occasion a Design Technology teacher received a written warning when he attended Wimbledon Quarter Final Day instead of attending an OCR Examination Board inset. Another written warning was presented to Miss Digit of the Mathematics Department for kissing the Head Boy after he won the javelin competition in the Lord Bilgebury Sports Day. It didn't seem to be of interest to anyone that the boy in question was Danny Digit, Miss Digit's younger brother. Unfortunately there was nothing incriminating in the file of David Fotheringay.

However, I was quite interested to read the contents of Augustine Slabb. It turns out that he has a Chemistry degree from the University of Nottingham and before he decided upon his present vocation he was an industrial chemist with ICI. Indeed he didn't become a cleric until he was late into his thirties. Of course he is not alone in joining the teaching profession quite late on. Many people who have failed in other fields are normally quite happy to become teachers and fail in the world of education too. They see it as a job for life with a reasonable salary, long holidays and a short working day.

Also, very few poor teachers are removed from their posts – fortunately.

Every Tuesday evening Miranda Slabb leaves Primrose Cottage to offer comfort to those sleeping rough on the streets of Cambridge. I am sure the vagrants would prefer to be left well alone as far as Miranda Slabb is concerned. According to Augustine she regularly deprives them of their cheap gin on a Tuesday evening and instead offers them the healthier delights of carrot juice. The absence of Miranda Slabb from Primrose Cottage induced me to visit my old friend, the Chaplain. I was rather hoping he had spare tickets for the forthcoming test series against South Africa. As I was shown into the inner sanctum of the Slabb abode I couldn't help but notice a strange and unpleasant smell.

'Good grief, Slabby. What on earth is that stink? Has Miranda changed her perfume or something?'

'No it's just something bubbling away in my study.'

'Odd place to boil your cabbage. Does the mistress of the house not allow you to use the kitchen?'

'I am not cooking anything Sebastian. It's merely an experiment with my chemistry set.'

'I didn't know you were interested in chemistry, Slabby.' I lied, but I didn't want him to know I had been snooping in his file.

'I like to dabble when I get the chance, and of course Tuesday evening is the perfect time with Miranda in the city centre looking after the down and outs.'

While Augustine was making coffee in the kitchen I made myself comfortable in his study. I have to say I was very impressed with his range of interests. On his desk there were the expected books on religion, but there was other reading material on topics such as the America Civil War, the inventions of Barnes Wallis, plants of South America and there was even an old book on frogs of the world. It was all very impressive.

I have always enjoyed my chats with the Chaplain. He was still very unhappy about the ending of cricket at Lord Bilgebury the following year, but he remained convinced that Grover-Smythe would have a U-turn on the issue. The time was approaching ten o'clock and it occurred to me that Miranda Slabb would soon be returning to Primrose Cottage. Not wishing to come across her in the dark I left the company of my friend without any test match tickets.

The following day I received a phone call from Wayne Flack. He had decided that in view of recent developments, he would take a gap year. I assumed correctly he did not intend to involve himself in any worthy causes such as teaching English to the impoverished youth of Peru or digging wells in Uganda. Wayne's plan, instead, was to spend several months visiting a selection of notorious locations such as Amsterdam, Bangkok and Rio de Janeiro. Colombia may also hold some interest for him. In the meantime I was to ensure 'he' passed his History exam in the following January session. He also suggested I could make a financial contribution toward his travel arrangements. I was reluctant to hand over any money, but the idea of having him out of the country for a few months was very appealing. I made arrangements to transfer two thousand pounds into his bank account. It seemed like a very shrewd investment. I also made contact with Courtney Brewer to ensure there were no other mishaps with regard to Wayne's exams. If, however, Wayne was foolish enough to visit Bali on his grand tour, I would make every effort to ensure he never left the island alive!

I was still considering the best way of dealing with David Fotheringay when I learned of a staggering development that unexpectedly resolved the issue for me. On the Monday morning, two weeks before the end of the Summer Term, Lucy Dockett informed me the Headmaster wanted to see me as a matter of urgency. I was to drop everything!

What I was to hear from Grover-Smythe was nothing short of incredible. I sat motionless as the Headmaster explained how on the previous Friday, Fotheringay, an English teacher in his spare time, decided to show his Year 10 class a short film on Shakespeare's *Merchant of Venice*. Exasperated by the fact his classroom computer would not work, he opted for using his school laptop to show the film. After starting the film Fotheringay left the classroom to pick up some work from his office. Whilst he was away an adult movie, which had been saved to the laptop by Fotheringay at home, started to play. By the time he returned to the classroom, and realised to his horror what had happened, the damage had been done. Apparently, he then asked the class to forget what they had seen and proceeded to play the Shakespeare film.

Lucy Dockett arrived at work this morning to discover that a number of angry parents had sent emails and left phone messages demanding that action be taken. One parent was so appalled they had already reported it to the social services. Another parent had also reported the incident to the *Cambridge Evening News*. No doubt the national press would soon also get hold of the story.

Grover-Smythe had already spoken to Fotheringay before I was asked to attend the Headmaster's Study. Fotheringay confirmed the events as described by Grover-Smythe. There was no alternative but to suspend the Deputy Headmaster while further disciplinary measures were considered by the Headmaster and the Board of Governors.

The fall of Fotheringay in such dramatic circumstances represented yet another body blow to the beleaguered Headmaster. Scandal was rampant at Lord Bilgebury College, and one wondered for how long the Headmaster himself could survive. As far as I was concerned, I hoped it would not be for much longer. Of concern, however, was the parental reaction to the shameful events that had rocked the College. Since the Ferret terrorist and espionage affair, there had been a steady flow of parents giving notice that they intended to withdraw their children from the College. This latest scandal to beset the College was very likely to turn the flow of parental notices to leave into a torrent. I now had to tread very carefully as I didn't want to become Headmaster of a school that was in imminent danger of closing. I was not going to become the Admiral Doenitz of Lord Bilgebury College! For the uneducated, Admiral Doenitz became leader of the Third Reich upon the suicide of Adolf Hitler in April 1945. Doenitz was not to last too long himself, and within twenty three days of assuming power he was deposed by the victorious allied forces!

For once I was blameless. Indeed I was regarded by the Headmaster and the governing board as a beacon of hope for Lord Bilgebury College. On the Tuesday morning I was appointed Deputy Headmaster.

20

The Senior Common Room was in a state of shock following the departure of Fotheringay. He appeared to be destined for high office in the world of academia. Most observers thought he would aspire to the headship of somewhere like Marlborough College or Winchester. Now, however, his career was in tatters and the best he could hope for was a position as Head of English in a minor public school.

I do not think I was the most popular choice to replace Fotheringay as far as my colleagues were concerned. I am sure they felt I had not been at the College long enough. At least to my face, however, they wished me well in my new position if only to ingratiate themselves in the eyes of the second most important member of staff. Augustine Slabb was being sincere when he offered me his congratulations. Sitting in the corner of the Common Room, he assured me of his support and furnished me with a ticket for the England versus South Africa one day international to be played at the Oval at the end of August, which he just happened to have in his inside jacket pocket.

'Thank you very much indeed, Slabby. I'll look forward to that. What are you reading there?'

'Usual stuff – Homer's *Iliad*.' Slabb removed his reading glasses to engage in conversation.

'You and your Greek mythology. I'm dipping into that new biography of Lloyd George at the moment. It's a pretty good read. He was a bit of a rogue you know.'

'Sebastian, you will try and use your good offices to do something about keeping cricket at the College?' Perhaps the Chaplain was less sincere than I thought.

'Don't worry, Slabby. I'll see what I can do.' Satisfied with my response, Augustine returned to Homer.

Following my appointment as Deputy Head the College was in need of a new Head of History. I was now going to be far too busy engaged in suspending and expelling miscreant youths and reprimanding colleagues for unprofessional conduct to be bothered with such mundane tasks such as actual teaching. The advertisement for the new head of department appeared in the *Times Educational Supplement* the following Friday. I received a call from Lucy Dockett the following Tuesday to inform me there had already been a couple of applications. As I had nothing better to do I decided to take a look at the applications of those who hoped to succeed me.

The first application form was pushed to one side as the applicant, a Mr Derek Dish, was currently residing in the county of Lincolnshire. I had no issue with anyone living in Lincolnshire especially as it was Grantham that gave us the late and lamented Baroness Thatcher. However, Mr Dish was married and unfortunately there was no married quarters available on the College campus and the cost of property in and around Cambridge was way above the national average, and certainly higher than Lincolnshire. I knew from experience he could not afford to live and work in Cambridge. I turned my attention to the other application form. Almost immediately there was a sense of panic and fear; Lucy Dockett noticed I had suddenly turned very pale. I was aware of a minor trembling all over my body. At the top of the application form for the Head of History position at Lord Bilgebury College was the name of Brian Fagg!

By courtesy of *The Times* I had always been aware that Fagg had survived the Underground accident and that he was unable to remember anything about the incident. Even if he was to recover his memory he would know only that a man called Richard Plantagenet was behind him on the station platform. However, if he were to see me in the flesh his recollection of events could be more than a little awkward.

Unfortunately Grover-Smythe had already seen the Fagg application and once again had been very impressed with the contents. He was determined to invite Fagg for an interview and, as Deputy Head, I was expected to be a part of the selection process. This would have represented too much of a risk and I had to find a way of not being in the vicinity of the College when the interviews were taking place. Of course there was a real possibility that Fagg would be successful in his quest to find employment at Lord Bilgebury. I was already entirely aware of his impressive credentials. However, I was confident I could thwart his ambitions from a safe distance.

There was a short-list of three candidates with the interviews taking place on Friday, 22 June. I had managed to persuade Grover-Smythe that I had to miss the interviews in order to honour a commitment to take my Year 12 students to *Chartwell*, the country home of Winston Churchill, in the Weald of Kent. Once again my sense of duty was applauded by the Headmaster, especially as I had suggested there was no better judge of character than he when it came to choosing the right candidate to fill the not insubstantial shoes of Sebastian Punknowle.

On the day of the interviews we made an early start for *Chartwell* to ensure I avoided bumping into Brian Fagg. I was hoping to arrive at Chartwell at about 11.00am to procure a coffee but we were delayed at the Queen Elizabeth II Bridge, which crosses the Thames at Dartford. A rather large lorry with a German number plate had bumped into a small car bearing a Polish number plate. Another case of history repeating itself! Also, as we entered the town of Westerham we stopped for a moment to admire statues of Churchill

and General James Wolfe, the victor of Quebec in 1759.

Upon reaching Chartwell and viewing the house for the first time one of my Year 12 charges, by the name of Wilberforce Dimmer, was unimpressed.

'Is that it then?' I think the boy was expecting to find something with more grandeur. I suppose he had a point. The house was hardly attractive – a Victorian red-brick country manor. I did point out to the group that the house commanded spectacular views across the Weald of Kent. Indeed it was because of the stunning scenary that Churchill purchased the property in 1922. Wilberforce Dimmer remained unimpressed.

I decided to give the group an hour of free time to investigate the house and grounds. It would give me an opportunity to think about the Brian Fagg situation should he be offered the job. However, I could not concentrate on the Fagg question. Instead I found myself engrossed in the Churchillian experience. I could imagine the great man in the 1930s walking from the house down to the extensive grounds to the man-made lake where, more likely and not, he would ponder on how to depose Stanley Baldwin or Neville Chamberlain as prime minister. I was becoming aware of how similar the experiences were of Punknowle and Churchill. I walked back to the house and sat on the wall of the back terraced garden and admired the views of this little corner of England.

I found myself considering the Churchill record and how I might incorporate him into my book on historical myths.

Quite rightly Churchill is regarded as the greatest Briton thus far. Sebastian Punknowle has yet to make his mark on history. When Britain stood alone against Nazi Germany in 1940, Churchill became the very embodiment of Britain's determination to resist. When Britain emerged victorious in 1945 many around the world credited Churchill with the demise of Hiterism. Those at home in Britain were less generous in their support and gratitude and duly elected into power a Labour Government.

When analysing historical characters I am a great believer in considering the psychology of the individual. Historical sources and documents can only reveal so much and they do not necessarily inform us of what some people actually think. There are those who could not possibly record what they thought because it would be too damning for them to do so.

There can be little doubt that Churchill wanted his place in history as the heroic defender of the British race in the Second World War. But if there had been no war then Churchill's record would have been less impressive and certainly no more heroic than any other mediocre Cabinet minister on the twentieth century. It was the Second World

War that made Churchill prime minister and only the continuity of the War would have enabled him to remain as the King's First Minister. I therefore believe that Churchill deliberately prolonged the war for his own selfish ends. When the French stopped fighting in the June of 1940, Britain's situation was desperate with invasion and defeat looking inevitable. Remarkably, Hitler offered Britain a way out of the dismal predicament by way of a seemingly generous peace proposal. Some members of the Cabinet such as the Foreign Secretary, Lord Halifax, urged Churchill to accept the lifeline. As we know Churchill refused, preferring to fight on until such a time when the British were choking in their own blood upon the ground. Churchill was entirely aware that such a surrender would not make good reading in the pages of history.

Churchill was also not in favour of Operation *Overlord*, the D-Day assault of the beaches of Normandy in June 1944. Churchill had a terrible row with the Yanks over the issue. The Americans believed that an Allied invasion of northern France would shorten the war due to its closer proximity to the Ruhr industrial area of western Germany. Churchill on the other hand advocated an Allied advance up through Italy with the aim of attacking southern Germany via the Alps and Austria. Churchill claimed he feared the huge number of Allied casualties with a cross-Channel assault. However, it is possible to suggest that Churchill preferred the Italian option because the War, and his premiership, would have gone on for longer.

I enjoyed my little excursion to *Chartwell*, but now it was time to return to the present and for my own plans for the pages of history. Whilst enjoying an ice cream I had received a text message from Grover-Smythe informing me that Brian Fagg and been by far the best candidate and that he would be offered the job as Head of History. I knew this could never be allowed to happen as too much was at stake. Whilst negotiating the M25 and M11 motorways I set my mind to work on how to once more neutralise the threat posed by Brian Fagg.

Upon my return to Lord Bilgebury there was no time to relax after my day in Kent. After a shower I immediately made my way to the railway station to catch the 1908 to Liverpool Street. The journey southwards to the capital was relatively uneventful and just before 9 o'clock I was able to emerge from the Oxford Circle tube station from where I made my way by foot to Tisbury Court in Soho. I did not feel at all comfortable in this seedy area but it was necessary for me to venture into the very epicentre of the London sex industry in order to achieve my objectives. Whilst on the train from Cambridge I had already identified the nature and location of my final destination in Tisbury Court. It did not take me long to find what I was looking for – *The Blue Lagoon Adult Shop.*

Before entering the sex shop I nervously looked around just to make sure that I didn't recognise anyone. I knew this would be unlikely but there was no harm in just making sure. Confident that all passers-by were complete strangers to me I nervously entered the shop. I had never seen anything like it in my life. There was an array of curious looking objects designed to give pleasure in the bed and, I assumed, up against the wall and presumably elsewhere in the privacy of one's home. Courtney Brewer would have been in heaven here. The shop was dominated by leather items including collars, whips and odd looking masks. In the middle of the shop floor there was a medieval torture rack with a price tag of five thousand pounds. There were other items on display which are too distasteful to describe but as far as I was concerned they represented physical impossibilities.

I had absolutely no intention of hanging around and quickly collected five items, which included one of those strange leather masks, a mouth gag, leather whip, wrist restraints and a black coloured dildo. I ventured to the counter and urged the sales assistant to deal with the transaction as quickly as possible. The young lady at the till reacted to my next request as if it was quite normal. I had asked that the items be put in a box and sent to the address, which I had written on a piece of paper. A receipt bearing the name of the customer would be placed in the box. The address I gave was for Lord Bilgebury College although the name of the recipient was omitted. The receipt in the box was made out to Brian Fagg! Eager to be away from the metropolis I was able to catch the 2255 train from Liverpool Street back to Cambridge.

The following Tuesday just before lunch I was summoned to the Headmaster's study. I proceeded without delay. Upon entering Grover-Smythe's office I viewed on his desk an opened cardboard box. With an absence of any addressee, Lucy Dockett and opened the package from the *Blue Lagoon Adult Shop* to reveal Brian Fagg's sex toys.

'Well Sebastian, what are we going to do about this one?' By this time Grover-Smythe had had his fill of scandal. I pretended to deliberate and then articulated my opinion on the matter. 'My view is that it would be very unwise to employ Mr Fagg. I am certain we have a duty, Headmaster, to protect our pupils.' Grover-Smythe nodded his approval of my assessment of the situation. I continued. 'Headmaster, fortunately we have yet to send any contract to Mr Fagg (I had previously been asked to check the wording but I had retained it in my desk drawer awaiting the parcel to arrive). Would you like me to phone him to say his services will no longer be required?' Grover-Smythe looked at me appreciatively. 'Oh Seb, would you mind? That's so awfully kind of you. Thank you.'

That evening I phoned Brian Fagg. I didn't mention the contents of the box and merely stated that the College now had plans to restructure the History Department and appoint from within. He accepted the decision with good grace but was obviously very disappointed. Arnold Pryke was to be surprised by his own elevation.

21

During the following Wednesday afternoon I went along to the Assembly Hall where the external examinations were taking place. The GCSE Biology exam had just started. Only about half of the candidates were taking their exam in the conventional way. The other half were depending upon readers, scribes, laptops and twenty five per cent extra time. I have always found these concessions a little ridiculous. How are these young men and women going to cope in the work place? Imagine a situation where someone in a busy office has to draft a letter or write a report. Would they ask their superior to find someone else to write it for them? If a report was needed in an hour, would they ask for extra time to complete it? In all probability they would be sacked. Under timed conditions many pupils with educational needs are able to type more words on a laptop than a gifted student can write with a pen. And, the pupil with a laptop gets twenty-five percent more time! Also, in order to be granted these generous concessions the parents have to pay around five hundred pounds for an educational psychologist's report. Not too many parents of the pupils from the local comprehensive can afford such a facility! This corrupt system gives an advantage to the wealthy. It's a way of keeping the great unwashed away from the best universities and well-paid jobs. On the other hand the system allows the slow, stupid and rich in our society to aspire to lucrative, but highly inappropriate, professions. I love it!

There is an expectation that examinations should be conducted in such a way that they comply strictly with the regulations and guidelines. Throughout my career I have always striven to evade such tiresome restrictions. For example, I advised my less-honourable History candidates in the recent examination to write a series of notes on their thighs. In this way, if they struggled to remember the facts, they simply requested to go to the toilet, lock the door, and take down their trousers to reveal the reasons for Napoleon Bonaparte's rise to power. On my way out of the Assembly Hall I did notice there was a pretty lengthy queue for the one and only lavatory.

I do like Wednesday afternoons, especially in the summer term. When most of the rest of the population are hard at it working in factories, down the mines, in offices, in hospitals or working on the roads, the teacher in an independent school can usually wander around the boundary watching a school cricket match in the sunshine. My companion on this particular Wednesday afternoon was the Reverend Slabb. The Lord Bilgebury College First XI was playing their local arch rivals, Saffron Walden School. Saffron Walden had set a total of 176, and in reply the College were in a spot of trouble at 113-6. Peter Turner, the umpire, would have his work cut out to ensure there were sufficient wides and no balls to secure a victory for the home team.

'How could the Headmaster even think about dropping cricket at the College? I mean, we would have to resort to watching the boys running round in circles on a Wednesday afternoon. Or, even worse, we might even be expected to watch females play rounders.'

'Don't worry yourself, Slabby. I'm sure cricket will continue here.'

'Oh I know it will, Sebastian. Have no fear about that.' Once more Slabb was going on the offensive. But surely he couldn't be aware of my plan to replace Grover-Smythe by the start of the next academic year.

'You know I will do my best Slabby, but what makes you so sure about the future of cricket?'

'That man will not be here next summer, Sebastian. Believe me, I know!' Had Slabb guessed what I was up to? Did he know something I didn't? Perhaps he had spoken to the Chairman of Governors about Grover-Smythe's future at the College.

'How do you know he will not be here?'

Augustine Slabb smiled, 'The will of God, old boy. The will of God.'

The College managed to beat Saffron Walden School by one wicket much to the disgust of their coach, who refused to speak to Peter Turner after the match. After the opposition had stormed off in their minibus, Peter admitted that thirty-eight questionable no-ball decisions may have aided Lord Bilgebury in their quest for the necessary runs. A hint of Bilgebury gin or vodka in the orange squash during the drinks interval may also have had a marginal effect upon proceedings. I walked back alone to the boarding house wondering at what stage I had hinted to Augustine Slabb about my intentions. On arriving home I sat down with a glass of chilled Pinot Grigio and studied Grover-Smythe's staff file. The final stage in the grand plan had begun.

The end of the academic year is always hard work for most teachers – in terms of finding something constructive to do. As Year 11 and Year 13 pupils normally finish their exams by the end of the third week in June, teachers have to cope with a limited teaching timetable for the last few weeks of the summer term. It can therefore be such a bore unless, like me, you can watch the test match on the telly all day. On Tuesdays, however, I still had a double Year 12 lesson, and therefore by the evening I was in need of some relaxation. On this particular evening my relaxation came in the form of reading my Lloyd-George biography.

I was enjoying my read with the occasional slurp of a decent claret when I reached an intriguing paragraph on page 297. I put down my wine glass and re-read the paragraph. After some deliberation I decided to phone Augustine Slabb just after seven o'clock with the intention of inviting him over to for a glass of red wine. As it was Tuesday evening I knew Miranda would be out tormenting the Cambridge homeless. However, no-one answered the phone, and I returned to my book and claret, but I could not progress past page 297.

Shortly afterwards the sound of sirens close by caused me to venture out to the main part of the College. There were police cars and an ambulance with their flashing blue lights by the main College entrance. At first I was denied access to the entrance by two uniformed police officers, until I convinced them of who I was. Without knocking I walked straight into the Headmaster's study to find a scene of mayhem. There were police officers, paramedics and slumped in his chair, being attended to, was Grover-Smythe.

'What on earth has happened here?' I was genuinely shocked by what I saw.

'Hello, Seb', the Headmaster was able to respond for himself, 'I'm afraid I've been attacked by an intruder. He tried to stick a hyperbolic needle in me, but fortunately I was able to fight him off and he ran away.'

'Do you know who it was?'

'Absolutely no idea, Seb. He was wearing a hood or balaclava or something. Dressed completely in black.'

The police forensic team continued to go about their business whilst the ambulance took Grover-Smythe to Addenbrooke's hospital for a check-up. When the police were still there I asked Peter Turner and Russ Dicker to calm the College down after all the excitement. I decided upon a stroll to Primrose Cottage. It was still only just after nine o'clock and therefore Miranda Slabb would still be out.

Slabb said he was unaware of the attack upon Grover-Smythe; he claimed had been at home since about six o'clock.

'Did you not hear your phone ring at about seven, Slabby? I called you then. I wanted to invite you over for some wine.'

'No, I didn't hear the phone. I had probably nodded off. Oh, I know, I was having a bath at that time.' A good try but I wasn't convinced. Slabb looked at me nervously. I simply had to come out with it.

'Slabby, why did you try to kill Grover-Smythe this evening?'

'What do you mean? That's absolutely absurd.' The Chaplain was starting to perspire.

'I don't think so, Slabby. I phoned you earlier because I had been reading my book on Lloyd-George. During the First World War, according to the book, there had been a plot to assassinate him.'

'What's that got to do with me?'

'They meant to kill him with a paralytic poison, but the attempt was thwarted by the British Secret Service.'

'I still don't understand what this has to do with me, Seb.'

'Slabby, my friend, when I was here last, on your desk in your study there was a book on South American plants and another on frogs of the world. There are plants in South America that produce curare, a poison used by the indigenous tribes for arrow heads or darts. The poison causes death by paralyzing the respiratory system, resulting in asphyxiation. But you know this already. Just as you know that the secretions of the South American black-legged dart frog also produce a deadly poison used by tribes for blow darts. Before you came to Lord Bilgebury, Slabby, you worked with a number of tribes in Colombia. You probably learned the potential of these poisons when you were there. Also, everyone knows you are a lover of mythology. Poisoned arrows are featured all over the place, including in the *Iliad*. I think I'm right in saying that both Achaeans and Trojans used poisoned arrows and spears. I'm sure if the police were to search Primrose Cottage they would find plenty of evidence linking you to these poisons and the murder of Donald Read, not to mention the attempted murder of Grover-Smythe.' Slabb had made no attempt to interrupt me. He had been rumbled and he knew it. There were tears in his eyes.

'Both of them wanted to destroy cricket, Seb. I couldn't let it happen. I went back to Colombia just over two years ago for a reunion with the Embera Choco tribe. I brought back the poisons then. I thought that if Miranda became too much, I could put myself out of my misery. I never intended to use it on anybody else. But Read and Grover-Smythe had to be got rid of.'

'A bit drastic, old boy.'

'Oh Seb, what must you think of me? What will Miranda think of me? This will destroy her.' This would be another positive outcome of this grisly affair.

'These things happen, Slabby.' He appeared perplexed by my response.

'What happens now? I suppose you will have to call the Police?'

'Certainly not.' He was even more perplexed.

'Well, what are you going to do Seb?'

'Absolutely nothing.'

'I beg your pardon?' I wasn't aware the Chaplain was hard of hearing.

'I said I'm going to do absolutely nothing. No-one need know about this. What you need to do now is get rid of any evidence. You haven't got any frogs hopping about the place, have you?' I was assured there were not.

'I don't know what to say, Seb. Why are you doing this?'

'No matter. But whatever happens in the future, I will demand your absolute loyalty and support.'

'You have my word, Seb.'

'Good. Now hurry up and deal with any incriminating evidence. And I shall be your alibi for the time when you attacked Grover-Smythe. If anyone asks, you were at my residence having a glass of wine when the attack took place.'

I went back home via Grover-Smythe's study. The forensic team had left but there was a police officer outside his door. There was also a policeman at the main entrance. When I returned home I phoned Addenbrooke's Hospital to be informed that Grover-Smythe was fine, but would stay in hospital overnight merely as a precaution. Had Slabb not been so clumsy, I may have been at least Acting Headmaster by now.

22

Grover-Smythe didn't come into the College on the Wednesday morning. It was decided that after his ordeal he should have at least the rest of the week off, and therefore I decided to run the College from his study. I received a number of visitors that morning. The first to call was Detective Inspector Sugden. He indicated that he wanted to interview all members of staff who lived on the College site. He also wanted his team to talk to all the sixth form boarders. It seemed certain the murder of Donald Read and the attack on Grover-Smythe were connected, and Sugden suggested the killer very probably had a link with the College. He wanted to read through all staff and pupil files, and this was to extend to the files of former teachers and past pupils. Fortunately, earlier that morning I had removed certain incriminating items from Slabb's file.

Sugden's request to go through the files suggested that he had absolutely no idea as to the identity of the culprit. It also seemed likely that the police forensic team had come up with very little or nothing at all in the way of clues. Slabb had obviously been very careful to cover his tracks, even in the process of fleeing the scene. However, he did point out that he was aware of the nature of the poison that had been used to kill Read in November. Before he departed I was asked the inevitable question and I responded that I was sharing a bottle of wine with the Chaplain at the time of the attack upon Grover-Smythe.

My next visitor that morning was the Chairman of Governors, Sir Fletcher Snogworthy. As he was more important than Sugden, I asked Lucy Dockett to organise some coffee and a plateful of superior biscuits. Before the shortbread arrived he helped himself to a seat on the sofa. He came straight to the point.

'Punknowle, I have been talking to some other members of the Board this morning. This is not generally known, but a few days ago, Walter came to see me to say he wanted a suitable financial package that would enable him to retire early. No-one can deny the man has gone through a rough patch recently and I indicated that the Board would look favourably on such a deal. We both felt that next December would be a good time for him to leave the College, and give the Board sufficient time to find a suitable replacement. However, after the events of last night, the Board feels that if he wants to, Walter should be allowed to retire with immediate effect and with a generous retirement package. Now, Punknowle, should Walter agree to the idea, how do you feel about taking on the role of Acting Headmaster?'

I was stunned; I didn't expect it to be this easy. 'I would be honoured to do it.' That was the best I could manage. The alternative was to stand before him like a speechless and dumb idiot.

'Of course, if things work out well, then I see no reason why you couldn't do the job on a permanent basis. If, however, it all goes pear-shaped, we'll have to consider someone else. Well, that's all settled then.' It took him two gulps to finish his coffee and then he was off to visit Grover-Smythe. Just after lunch I received a call from Sir Fletcher. Grover-Smythe had agreed to the package and would retire with immediate effect.

Upon receiving the news, I sat and stared at the ceiling. I then caressed the top of the Headmaster's desk – my desk. I was reminded of that historic moment on 10 May 1940, when Winston Churchill was appointed Prime Minister. Like him, I too felt as if I was walking with destiny and I was sure I would not fail. There was a knock at the door. Without any invitation to proceed, Detective Inspector Sugden presented himself on my carpet with two other police officers.

'Sebastian Punknowle.'

'Yes, what is it, Inspector?'

'You are under arrest for the murder of Dr Donald Read and the attempted murder of Walter Grover-Smythe. Sergeant Prickley, read him his rights.'

23

My trial began on Monday, 2nd November. Denied bail I had been detained in Bedford Prison since my arrest in late June. I was innocent of the crimes of which I had been accused, and as soon as I am acquitted, I will haul the Cambridgeshire Constabulary before the courts for wrongful arrest. Of course I have said nothing about Slabb's involvement in the murder of Read or the attempted murder of Grover-Smythe. There has been no need to. He is my main defence witness and the truth will soon be out – at the time Grover-Smythe was attacked, we were having a glass of claret. In effect we have a mutual alibi. Indeed, the Chaplain came to the Prison to see me last week and I was assured all will be well. My arrest had made the national news; the day after I had been taken into custody my picture was on the front page of *The Daily Reflector* – a dreadful rag read by the lower classes. The details of the case also featured on the BBC Breakfast News. I could well imagine Aunt Mildred spluttering over her cornflakes back at the farmhouse in Somerset.

Throughout this travesty of justice, I have been treated like a common criminal. I am forced to wear a grey prison uniform, which seems to indicate to the resident criminal classes that I have some sort of parity with them. I am surprised the authorities don't shave my head and be done with it. My cell is dreadful. I think my mattress must be filled with an assortment of rocks and my sheet and blanket are no larger than a table napkin. I wake up each morning facing the lavatory that has no seat, which I am required to clean each day. The food is terrible and almost on a par with Angelica Smite's tasteless offerings at Lord Bilgebury College. It is bad enough that I am required to eat with the criminal classes, but I am also forced to share my ablutions with them, and my request for an ensuite shower facilty was refused.

Apart from Augustine Slabb, my other regular visitor had been my barrister. Having spent most of my available cash on Wayne Flack's quest for academic success, I was obliged to seek legal aid. I was therefore not surprised when Piers Amhurst appeared in the prison interview room. The person who had the task of securing my acquittal was in his midtwenties and I was to be his very first brief. However, I was not too concerned as the case against me was so very weak. Also, if things ever looked bleak I was quite prepared to spill the beans with regard to Augustine Slabb.

I of course pleaded not guilty to the charges as set out by the Clerk of the Court. The scene before me as I sat in the dock was something out of the eighteenth century. In addition to the prosecution and defence lawyers, there was a proliferation of individuals with wigs. Of all the wigs on show within Number Two Court of the Cambridge County Court, the wig of my barrister was the whitest. The Judge, who looked as if he should have been pensioned off several years ago, was dressed in red. Before him there was a laptop. I suppose if he ever became bored with proceedings he could always book his holiday to Barbados online or play a game of patience. Talking of patience, I nearly lost mine when my barrister informed me that Augustine Slabb would not be first to go into the witness box. I wanted the trial to be over as quickly as possible and get back to running Lord Bilgebury College. The Slabb alibi would certainly clear my name; I was somewhat surprised it hadn't done so already.

The Prosecution produced an array of expert witnesses who droned on about various poisons that had their origins in South America. The Judge, and indeed my young defence counsel, appeared fazed by the testimony of a professor from University College, London, who went on and on about the curare poison.

'Knowledge of the poison became known in the fifteen hundreds – about the same time as chocolate and cocoa.'

The Judge then interrupted with a degree of concern, 'Are you saying Professor that my milky cocoa may be poisonous?'

'No, Your Lordship. I merely make the point that cocoa emerged at the same time as curare.'

'Professor, please refrain from wasting the Courts time on trivia.'

After apologizing, the expert witness continued, 'The chemical compound took around three hundred years to develop having first discovered the extract and the plant. The pure compound was isolated and eventually removed from the Chondrodendron and synthesised. The physiological action of the poison is the blocking of acetylcholine at the neuro-muscular junction.'

The Judge was confused, 'What exactly does that mean?'

'It means death, Your Lordship.'

It was apparent how Slabb's former life in the chemical industry was of use to him in the planning and execution of his murderous deeds. I, of course knew virtually nothing about poisonous trees and frogs.

I was a little surprised when Wayne Flack appeared as a prosecution witness. His testimony could do me a good deal of harm. The prosecuting barrister asked Wayne to tell the Court about the events of Monday, 14th November, the day before Read's murder.

'I was in 'is flat weren't I.'

'In the flat of Sebastian Punknowle?' The prosecuting barrister was seeking clarification for the Jury.

'Yeah, that's right.'

'What exactly were you doing in Mr Punknowle's flat?'

'It was lunch time weren't it. I was 'avin' a beer and watchin' *Neighbours*.'

'Did you do this often?'

'Yeah, suppose I did.'

'Was it not a little strange for a student to be having a beer in a teacher's flat at that time of day?'

'Suppose so, but he liked it. I reckoned he was a bit queer, but it didn't bother me too much.' The Judge raised an eyebrow.

'Can you tell the Court what happened that lunchtime, whilst you were watching television with beer in hand.'

'Noggins came to 'is door wantin' some dosh.'

'Then what happened?'

'Punknowle went to the office to get 'im some.

'And what did you do then?'

'Went to get another lager from the fridge, and I saw 'is computer screen on, so I read what was on it.'

'And what was on the screen? Remember, you are under oath.'

'He'd bin writin' a note saying he was goin' to do 'imself in.'

'Mr Punknowle was contemplating suicide?'

'No, not him – Dr Read.'

'Let's get this absolutely clear, Mr Flack. You are saying that Sebastian Punknowle drafted a suicide note from Dr Read?'

'Yeah, that's about it.'

The Jury looked at me as if they were prepared there and then to pronounce me guilty. I had done so much for Wayne, only for him to betray me in this way. Had he no honour? It was now the time for my young barrister to cross-examine Flack.

'Mr Flack, may I suggest you are not exactly a reliable witness.'

'Dunno what you're on about.

'Can you tell the court how you came to leave Lord Bilgebury College?

'I was asked to weren't I.'

The Judge interrupted before Amhurst could continue, 'Is this witness a former pupil at an English public school?' The prosecuting counsel responded that he was, 'Good heavens,' came the Judge's reply.

Amhurst was allowed to continue. 'And why exactly were you asked to leave, Mr Flack?'

'I 'it someone.'

'Mr Flack, you were expelled. You were expelled for torturing and bullying the younger boys. And it was Mr

Punknowle who was instrumental in your having to leave Lord Bilgebury. Quite simply you have a grudge against Mr Punknowle, don't you?

'That's crap!' Amhurst kept up the pressure.

'It is this grudge that has caused you to invent this lie about what you claim you saw on that computer. No-one else saw the screen, did they?

'Suppose not.'

'Why didn't you report what you saw to someone else, such as a teacher or the Headmaster?'

'Dunno.'

'You don't know. The reason you didn't tell anyone is because it was never there on the screen. This is all a fabrication; a malicious attempt to destroy the good name of Sebastian Punknowle. One more thing, Mr Flack. How much is the *Daily Reflector*' paying you for your story?' My defence team had done well. I knew Flack dare not bring up the Picton fire or the exam situation without incriminating himself and losing two A grade A levels.

The next witness to appear was Horace Smedley, the Crankton fete organizer. I assumed he was in Court as a character witness and to inform the jury of my generosity. I was wrong.

A rather smug-looking lawyer for the prosecution got to his feet to ask Smedley about the nature of the theft, and his response was not exactly helpful to my cause.

'When the charity money was stolen, Mr Punknowle offered to donate some money from his own pocket.' Nothing too damning there, I thought. Even the prosecution barrister seemed to agree.

'Surely, Mr Smedley, that was an act of generosity on the part of the defendant?'

'That's what I thought at first, but it was the amount of money he handed over.'

'And how much was that?'

'Two thousand, five hundred and twenty seven pounds.'

'A very generous amount.'

'Yes, but it was the exact same amount of money that had gone missing.'

'So what was so unusual about that?'

'Well, how did he know how much money had been stolen? I was the only person who knew. I had only just counted the takings and there was no way Mr Punknowle would have known.' This was an act of the utmost ingratitude on the part of Horace Smedley. I could have kept the money.

The following day the prosecution called Uncle Rex. I had not seen or heard from Uncle Rex since the day of the election in early May. I was a little upset he had not been in contact since my arrest. However, I couldn't see how he could be of any use to the prosecution side.

'I have known Sebastian all his life, especially so since the death of his parents nearly twenty years ago. Car accident, you know. Dreadful, absolutely dreadful.'

'Can I ask why you are here, Mr Punknowle?' The prosecution barrister smiled sympathetically.

'Matter of honour. Service in the Royal Air Force taught me that. Never forgotten it.'

'What exactly do you mean by matter of honour, Mr Punknowle?'

'It's the family name, you know. Been shamed.'

'By whom, Mr Punknowle?'

'By him. Him over there in the dock.'

'Sebastian Punknowle?'

'I cannot bear to utter his name. He has shamed the family.' What was he babbling on about?

'You mean his presence in Court and the crimes of which he has been accused?'

'Yes. And other things.' What other things?

'What other things, Mr Punknowle?' Uncle Rex hesitated before quietly responding.

'The fire.'

'The fire, Mr Punknowle. What fire?'

'The fire at Picton College. It is my belief that he, Sebastian, was responsible for the fire that destroyed a large part of the College.'

Amhurst rose to his feet. 'Your Lordship, Mr Punknowle is not on trial for starting any fires.'

'I am prepared to allow prosecution counsel to continue with their line of questioning. It may have a bearing on the defendant's character.'

'I am grateful to Your Lordship,' I'm not sure I was, 'Please continue, Mr Punknowle.'

'Last December, my nephew, Sebastian, was staying with us down in Somerset for the Christmas holidays. He was later joined by one of his pupils, Wayne Flack. Apparently he needed help with his revision. While they were there staying with us, Picton College went up in flames. I am the Chairman of the Governors there, and my nephew was a History teacher at the College until he was obliged to leave.'

'Would you explain why Sebastian Punknowle had to leave Picton College?'

'I'm afraid he was involved in a case of false accounting. I agreed with the Headmaster that my nephew should leave the College quietly. We didn't want a fuss you see.'

'Thank you, Mr Punknowle. Please continue.'

'When my nephew stood for election for the Cambridge District Council last May my son Perkin and I went up to Cambridge to lend Sebastian a hand. When we were there he made reference to the fact that the new desks and chairs had been destroyed in the fire.' There was now a pause, which allowed the prosecuting council to pursue his line of questioning.

'What was the significance of the issue over the desk and chairs at Picton College?' Uncle Rex looked up at me sitting grim-faced in the dock. He continued to look in my direction as he gave his answer to the question.

'Sebastian left Picton College a long time before the College received new desks and chairs. The refurbishment had been of so little interest that I had not even bothered to inform Sebastian about the new furniture. There is no way that he could have known about the new desks and chairs unless he had seen them for himself. He had not been back to the College since he left.'

'So let the Court be very clear about this. Are you suggesting that your nephew, Sebastian Punknowle, started the fire at Picton College?'

'Yes sir, I am afraid to say that I am.' I closed my eyes and hung my head. Piers Amhurst, however, was quick to cross-examine the treacherous Uncle Rex.

'Mr Punknowle, do you have any proof whatsoever that my client started the fire apart from these rather vague references to new furniture?'

'No, but how would he have known if he had not seen the desks and chairs for himself?'

'Is it not possible that someone who worked at the College, a teacher, perhaps, could have told my client about the new furniture? How can you be so sure you didn't tell him yourself?'

'I am sure I didn't.'

'Is it not possible, for example, that Wayne Flack, that paragon of virtue, started the fire, and that he mentioned to my client about the new furniture?'

'Well, I suppose it's possible, but…'

'Thank you Your Lordship. I have no more questions.' As the time was now just after four o'clock, the Judge decided to adjourn for the day. It had been a terrible day. However, there was still no evidence to suggest that I had killed Read or attacked Grover-Smythe. I knew I could rely on Augustine Slabb.

24

'I swear by Almighty God that the evidence I shall give, shall be the truth, the whole truth and nothing but the truth.' Augustine Slabb handed the Bible back to the Court Usher. I had never seen Slabb look so smart. He was not wearing his usual herringbone jacket with the lapels that had a mind of their own. There was no evidence on the front of his black clerical shirt to indicate what he had eaten, and missed, for breakfast. His dog collar was as white as white could be. He had obviously made every effort to impress the Court for the sake of his friend, Sebastian Punknowle. After confirming his name, Slabb was asked by Piers Amhurst to go through the events of the evening when Walter Grover-Smythe was attacked.

'My wife, Miranda, left home about six o'clock. As it was a Tuesday evening she was going into Cambridge city centre to give comfort to the homeless. Just before seven I went out to visit a friend of mine for a glass of sherry.' Surely he meant to say wine.

'With the defendant, Sebastian Punknowle?' There was an awkward pause.

'Actually no, I went to have a sherry with the Vicar of Shelford, just across the road from Lord Bilgebury College in the *Dog and Duck* public house.' Slabb looked nervously over at me sitting dumbfounded in the dock. Both defence and prosecuting counsels were astounded by Slabb's version of events. Once he had gathered himself, my barrister began to challenge the Lord Bilgebury Chaplain.

'In a signed statement to the Police you said that you had been with my client at the time the attack upon Mr Grover-Smythe took place. Can you explain this new version of events to the Court?'

'Over the past few months I have wrestled with my conscience. I regret to say that I lied to the Police because I wanted to protect a dear friend. I simply could not believe he could have done such a wicked thing. But I knew that I had to answer to a Higher Authority and that my conscience could not be at peace until I told the truth.'

'Did you see Sebastian Punknowle at all on that evening?'

'No, young man, I did not.' I could not believe my ears. How could he possibly get away with this rubbish? Surely, the Vicar of Shelford couldn't possibly confirm what Slabb had just said. Slabb was busily trying to murder Grover-Smythe at the time.

As a result of Slabb's testimony the Court was in a state of some ferment. The Judge agreed to my barrister's request for an adjournment to consult with his now embattled client. During the meeting with my barrister I informed him of what I knew about the activities of Augustine Slabb.

Back in Court, Amhurst continued to question Slabb. 'Is it not possible that you were the one responsible for the murder of Dr Donald Read and the attempted murder of Walter Grover-Smythe. You certainly had the motive and opportunity. Is it not true that you detested Read and Grover-Smythe because of their stance on cricket at Lord Bilgebury

College? You were angry because they both wanted to get rid of cricket at the College. Is that not the case Reverend Slabb?'

'I was not the only one to have reservations about the decision to take away cricket from the College. There are a number of my colleagues, including Sebastian, who share my views. Also, however much I love the wonderful game, I would never kill another human being to keep cricket alive and kicking at the College. After all, I am a man of God. Besides, I have already told you, I was having a glass of sherry with the Vicar of Shelford.'

'And what about the evening Dr Read was murdered. Were you having a glass of sherry with the Vicar of Shelford on that occasion as well?'

'No, I wasn't. As Miranda, my wife, was out I had supper in the Staff Dining Room at the time poor Donald Read was murdered. Peter Turner, our Physics teacher can confirm I was there for over an hour. Incidently I do not believe we had the pleasure of Sebastian's company at supper that evening – most unusual.'

'Reverend Slabb, would you kindly tell the Court about your interest in South American poisons.'

'I have absolutely no interest in such things. I only know what Sebastian has told me. Something to do with flowers and frogs I think. He borrowed a couple of my books on South America some months ago. He never returned them. He mentioned something about a poisonous frog at the time.'

'Whilst on the subject of South America is it true you spent a considerable period with the indigenous tribes of the Colombian jungle, the same tribes that produce poisons for their arrow heads?'

'No, certainly not. I spent all my time in Bogota, the capital. I never left the city and that can be confirmed by the Archbishop of Bogota. I can't stand the jungle, especially all those snakes and creepy crawlies. My wife, however, spent some time with the native tribes. She helped some of them to learn English, and she also worked very hard to set up a Sunday school.'

Slabb eventually left the witness stand. I had been double crossed, but I wasn't sure how he hoped to get away with so many false statements. Surely the Police would have to investigate his wild claims. Considering the nature of the new 'evidence' the Judge was persuaded to adjourn early for the day so that both defence and prosecution teams could make further consultations and enquiries.

The first person to take the stand the following morning was my arresting officer, Detective Inspector Sugden. The prosecution team opened the proceedings.

'Detective Inspector, can you take us through the events that led you to arrest the defendant, Sebastian Punknowle.'

'Yes sir. Following the attack upon the Headmaster of Lord Bilgebury College on Tuesday, 26th June of this year, my officers proceeded to search the premises of all the resident teaching and domestic staff of the College. My team, with the permission of the defendant, also searched the rooms of all sixth-form boarders.'

'And what, if anything, did you discover as a result of these searches, Detective Inspector?'

'When we entered the residence of Mr Punknowle, we discovered a liquid substance in the refrigerator. The substance was taken to the police laboratories for examination where they concluded it was the same poison that killed Dr Donald Read in the November of last year.'

'Did you find anything else in the residence?'

'Yes, we found a selection of books in the study that indicated sufficient research had been undertaken into poisonous plants and frogs of South America. A biography was on the coffee table open at page 297. A paragraph on the said page explained how Lloyd-George was nearly assassinated by means of a poison dart. Also, behind some books on the book shelf we found a blow pipe and a hypodermic syringe. Non-toxic darts were also discovered in a match box in Mr Punknowle's sock drawer.' With the exception of the Lloyd-George biography, the presence of these items were a mystery to me. They must have been planted there by Slabb, the scheming, treacherous toad. It was time for Amhurst to tackle the detective of police.

'Detective Inspector, the suggestion was made yesterday that the College Chaplain, the Reverend Slabb, may have been involved in the attack upon Walter Grover-Smythe. Was his residence, Primrose Cottage, searched with the same thoroughness as other properties on the College campus?'

'Yes sir.'

'And what did you find?'

'Absolutely nothing, sir.' It was me who suggested that Slabb remove the evidence. I didn't expect him to remove it to my house!

'What of Reverend Slabb's alibi?'

'The Vicar of Shelford confirms that he met the Reverend Slabb for a sherry at the *Dog and Duck* public house at the times indicated. There was no way he could have been anywhere near the Headmaster's study. There are other witnesses to confirm the Chaplain was in the pub.' This couldn't be true. Slabb admitted making the attack on Grover-Smythe. I didn't understand. I could tell Amhurst was losing hope. So was I.

'What about his alibi for the time Dr Read was murdered?'

'Both Peter Turner and Russ Dicker confirm Augustine Slabb was having supper with them on the evening of 15th November. They also confirm Mr Punknowle was not having supper with them.'

At this point my defence counsel slumped back into his seat. The barrister for the prosecution seemed to rise majestically from his seat.

'Detective Inspector, according to your records what was Sebastian Punknowle doing at the time of Dr Read's murder.'

'He claimed he visited Sainsbury's, sir. However, last night we went through all the CCTV records at every store in and around Cambridge between six and eight o'clock on the evening of 15th November. There was no sighting of Mr Punknowle entering any supermarket.' I was done for.

They were all there to hear the verdict. The recently retired Grover-Smythe was sitting next to Lucy Dockett, soon to be Mrs Grover-Smythe once his divorce had gone through. Tim Ferris, the Ferret was sitting next to his former headmaster, having been released by the United States authorities the previous July. Gloria Read was rather hoping I would be hanged. Theodore Clapp had walked into the public gallery with a slight limp. Uncle Rex and Aunt Mildred had come up from Somerset to witness the shame brought upon the house of Punknowle. Cousin Perkin, by all accounts, had preferred to re-enact the Battle of Stalingrad with some recently-procured soldiers. Wayne Flack was in attendance with a healthy smirk. He wouldn't be smiling for long. I would ensure the proper authorities be made aware of the conditions under which his examinations were taken. This would probably result in the dismissal of Courtney Brewer from his post, but I was past caring. Nancy Noggins was present of course. She reminded me of those old hags who sat knitting by the guillotine during the French Revolution. Last but not least the new Headmaster and his wife were there to witness the final humiliation of Sebastian Punknowle. The recently appointed new Headmaster, Augustine Slabb, ensured the game of cricket would continue to be played at Lord Bilgebury College.

I was found guilty of the murder of Donald Read and the attempted murder of Walter Grover-Smythe. The Judge sentenced me to twenty four years imprisonment.

25

Whilst in prison I learned of the death of Augustine Slabb. He had suffered a heart attack having just scored a half century against the Lord Bilgebury First XI. Miranda, his wife, soon followed him to the grave. Shortly before his death he had handed a sealed envelope to his solicitor and gave strict instructions that I should be sent the envelope upon the death of his wife, and not before. I received the sealed envelope three years into my sentence. The contents made for interesting reading.

My Dear Punknowle,

It is my sincere wish that upon receiving this letter you will be released from prison. We both know you were not guilty of the crimes for which you were accused. You may be interested to learn that I am not a murderer either. Unfortunately, the same could not be said of my beloved Miranda. She was always very ambitious for me.

At least cricket will thrive at Lord Bilgebury College!

Augustine Slabb signed the letter in his own hand. I was released from prison upon a successful appeal.